"I knew the bride when she used to rock n roll"

A Ghost Story
by

Ricky Dale

I knew the bride when she used to rock n roll

Published by Ricky Dale
Publishing partner: Paragon Publishing, Rothersthorpe
First published 2021

ISBN 978-1-78222-809-7

Book design, layout and production management by Into Print
www.intoprint.net
+44 (0)1604 832149

FOREWORD

Until you hear a snowflake fall
Or see a face upon a wall
Until your heart can't beat at all
What do we know about Life?

Until you feel you walk on air
Until there's always someone there
Until it's more than you can bear
What do we know about Life?

I HAD AN impulse to write a semi-fictional novel about the afterlife based upon some of my own experiences which I intended to throw into the pot as well. Although my encounters with the spiritual incidents were worldly rather than supernatural, nevertheless they were still quite intense.

I had an appealing storyline and plot already figured out. I envisaged basing the main story upon a novel I had read years ago. It concentrated upon a group of passengers aboard a fog en-shrouded crewless ship. At first they don't realise that they are in fact dead and had believed that they were all on a trip to America. Then, little by little, they begin to grasp that the one thing they all have in common is that they *are* dead and waiting to be judged for the afterlife and whether they will go to heaven or hell!

Although I had planned to prudently rework and, therefore, refashion the original gambit to give rise to a 21st century interpretation, it really went horridly pear-shaped when my research indicated the following:-

- *Outward Bound* the movie was first released in 1930
- *Between Two Worlds* the movie remake was released in 1944
- A *Twilight Zone* episode was available online
- Moreover, and to cap it all, *The Simpsons* had parodied the movie!!

With all of that in mind I am relieved to relate that this is positively the complete and unabridged version of *I knew the bride when she used to rock n roll* from the original manuscript!

I hope that you enjoy it!

Ricky Dale

CONTENTS

PREFACE

THE LAST ONE hundred years is an ocean upon which for some period of time we have all sailed. We remember its capricious moods, its storms and calms, its ups and downs, the pleasures along the way, but perhaps most of all the company of friends with whom we travelled.

Among this panoply of memories will surely be the resurrection of very personal memories. Memories which have become entombed in our psyche, memories which have moulded us into what we ourselves are.

We should never cease to search these memories out, to cherish each and every rare episode; for if not we are guilty of overwhelming ingratitude to those who created them. We will not only impoverish our own lives, but also deprive the creators of these memories their inheritance as well.

The 'friends' I have named are not fictional – it would be too sweet to write a story with 'made up' characters – 'my friends' are actual visitors, nothing more besides would do!

For example, when Molly and me visited New York it would have been a 'no-quibble' sequence of events to have had La Guardia visit us at The Taft. However, the fact that our 'visitor' was the lowly bellboy is the truthful account.

I have often speculated upon the accurate interpretation of what makes a book a book and what makes a novel a novel and, after some careful consideration, it seems to me that I think I know the answer. A book is something light and often unsubstantial whilst, on the other hand, a novel tends to be a serious work with perhaps something to say.

A similar distinction would be a book being entertainment of sorts, whilst a novel being simply a creation by my 'friends'.

Ricky Dale

This novel is dedicated to Molly:

"Obsessed by a fairy tale, we spent our entire lives searching for a magic door and a lost kingdom of peace"

– Eugene O'Neill –

WHEN IT ALL boils down, we can truly thank my daughter Molly for all of these freely written pages for all you fine folk to read. For it is her unrest and non-prevarication of words that has un-questionably formed the factual justification of this book.

All that I have pitched in here and there is some sort of cipher of metaphors and periodically provided the reader with a set of keys to unlock them.

Most of the wrinkles I have learned about the aesthetics of writing over the years I have long since forgotten, except that perhaps fundamentally it's all really about having some great and simple ideas and a well-sharpened pencil, that's all!

If you can then somehow find that writerly equilibrium then conceivably you may have a story; that's what I thought! How-ever, it wasn't until I came across Molly's discarded journal in amongst some books I was going to give to the charity shop, and it wasn't until I had flicked through the pages that I discovered the gravity of 'real' narrative. Molly had so meticulously documented everything of special interest and facets of our lives that I had dismissed long ago. Her cram packed pages painstakingly detailed every 'headstone'.

Dear Molly, you began this vestige of the incomprehensible and so now, with your agreement, I will add a smidgen of sem-blance and dash and make it my responsibility to draw it to a conclusion!

Dad

Does true love have a habit of coming back?
You decide!

– Denisa Comanescu –

1

Gays and Ghosts

HUMAN LIFE – the absurdity of it. The ignorance of it. The greatness of it. The intelligence of it. The profundity of it. When you are looking unsqueamishly at it, you are essentially looking at all of those things and more.

However, when you look at death it's nothing but absolute beauty is incorruptibly breathtaking. Perhaps because, although remorselessly dead, by default death is nevertheless incarnately very much still alive.

It seems to me that I haven't to date found that many 'still functioning' ghosts/spirits to engage with; not their fault though, whereas back in the late 1960s and early 1970s I had the opportunity to become acquainted with oodles of the heavenly breed. Once I had encouraged them to come on out of their closet (or cloister) it was as though they had truly reawakened.

Not unlike the gay individuals during the 1967 decriminalisation of gays, and of ghosts I am inclined to say – only if you were over 21 years of age that is – not so with ghosts though!

If truth be told I somewhat abandoned my dependable 'dead' cronies during the latter years of the 1970s – which was frightfully remiss and impolite of me. However, in mitigation, it was only because so many other priorities had taken over my life. For example, most notably I had ditched my 30 something wife in exchange for a 19 year old 'twinky' from the north and shamefully I had become a new age swinger and svengali!

Blinking like a miscreant owl, I awoke one morning doped out and readily realising that absolutely nothing and nothing more besides mattered more than my Molly and our erstwhile comforting spectrals.

After I had pulled through I discovered that that 'twinky' had not only misappropriated funds from my current account, but had also helped herself to Molly's – Molly was only four! I guess to that northern xxxxx (this word is generally only used in kennels!) Molly and me were just non-technical residuums of passing time!

> For love is only moments here and there
> It comes and goes quickly I think
> Often you hear it like silver bells
> Tied like a stranglehold about the throats of cats

The way things are now and according to reasoning the 'exciting' scenarios that follow are a frank and accurate account of how our 'friends', Molly and me interact on a daily basis – in home and family life. Particularly between the hours of 1am and 3am – and the in-between time of 4 'til 5.

> Odd things have been happening
> here for some time.
> It is peaceful, it is the flow
> of a non-transparent ripple
> that is guarded from both sides.

2

God Bless the Blues

"IT WAS A moonlit night in Old Mexico. I walked alone between some adobe haciendas. Suddenly I heard the plaintive cry of a young Mexican girl. La la la laa laa laa" etc etc.

My Molly especially adored the unorthodoxed opening to Pat Boone's ditty ie as above, but without the la, la, la's! She'd often assert that "it was a moonlit night" etc was a spooky song. "Put the spooky song on Dad; Speedy Gonzalo!" she'd say.

From Munich to Minnesota I think that children have always had a fascination with the freaky 'heebie jeebies'. That's not to say that they would relish having the living daylights scared out of them, however a little bit of the grim and the grisly, they actually get a buzz out of it. When years ago I used to tell my kid brother spooky tales at bed time, I remember him punctuating several paragraphs with an astonished "hot dog!"

Not so with Molly though. She neither got a kick out of spooky stuff, or was indeed frivolously frightened by anything creepy at all – although she would make as though she was frightened, it was all a sham. To my Molly it was all just a way of life – and I guess, so it was!

We've learned so much.
Everything, it seems,
But how to stay in touch?

'They' say that snails are a thousand times more clairvoyant than we are (I don't know how 'they' arrived at that supposition) and a rooster has the knack of cutting out all forgetfulness and yet between error and truth, between instinct and rationality, between a dead person and the live one, there is an uproar of silence when it comes to incorporeal issues – and there's really no need for it.

For example, you never know for certain which 'whatshisname' you are likely to communicate with at any given session. A chick you went out with somewhere back down the line, an old man with no name you spoke to in a town you don't remember. Any of them can appear from out of the past to trigger your blues or your delight – there is just no telling which it will be! Not entirely typical is an incident that came about quite unexpectedly. How awesome can it get to be one minute sat in your comfortable lounge in a tiny seaside town on the south coast of England and next minute you are conversationing way down below that mystic Mason-Dixon Line!

She was a pretty hot-tempered girl when I first began to speak to her – even called me a *'Mother Fucker'*, which I was not totally prepared for! She didn't give her name at first and referred to herself as a 'race' woman! However, Billie Holiday stayed in our home for over three months. I asked her a lot of stuff that she didn't give answers to. In spite of that she did imply that 'Strange Fruit' had transformed her career. There was often an irresolution or 'dilly dally' in her come backs – it was almost as though she was still able to embrace emotion. In my dealings with Billie and all of the others I always handled their messages with dignity and respect – the same as you should with a regular person!

3

Ego

MOLLY AND I never felt like we were alone – never felt it was wholly a prerequisite to close windows and doors because of the bogeyman. I would however cover the large mirror in the passageway from time to time as that was a different proposition entirely!

I guess that becoming acquainted with all of these fine folk made us feel good about ourselves, indeed it was 'good for our ego', but not like the hackneyed phrase might imply. What I am trying to explain is that being able to truthfully see life and death through someone else's perspective rather than my own was such a great privilege.

It was as though my newly found ego was translating how they (the spirit) felt through what I would feel in similar circumstances. It had become almost an instant reaction when hearing about the other persons tale of woe to turn inwards towards myself slightly.

Shadows offer safety in the dark
parts of the house.

4

Hamptonia/aka The Spooky House!

OUR HOME WAS a whopping very lived-in annexe to a rundown Victorian country house which had stood vacant for years.

My first wife and me had purchased the outmoded parsonage with the intention of renovating it into several residential homes. However, the city fathers considered our development plans too ambitious and reversed their earlier decision. By the Fall of 1967 business dictated that the old annexe became our home.

My wife had named it 'Hamptonia' after a thorougbred horse she had once owned. Several years later Molly and me renamed it 'The Spooky House' for obvious reasons.

From the outside I guess it was a depressing looking dark and forbidding type of building. It was set among several acres of entangled weeds and dead trees which we hadn't the resource to clear. It kind of appealed to me in a somewhat pseudo-romantic way, like it had somehow lost its purpose and belonged more properly in a Utopian Gothic novel.

The very first time I saw the place I remember squinting through my windscreen as I pulled up outside with mixed fear and reverence. I could so easily imagine that girl in a purple dress running to the cliff edge and the old house in the background with its shutters banging! However, once you stepped inside there was something rather endearing and enchanting about our 'Spooky House' as I will explain in due course.

In the evening
when silence has fallen
over everything
A thousand eyes sparkle
and look deeply
into mine.

In the same evening
when the wind scatters
through the house
A million unwritten words
left smouldering all day
sing out.

5

Martha Amersley

'WHAT KIND OF cigarettes did you smoke?' 'What kind of car did you drive?' 'What was your occupation?' Every ouija board gets asked these emaciated questions and every ouija has the erroneous answers – kind of like a defied compliance. Just once I'd like to hear some brand new smart questions. Asking questions of an ignoble nature is almost like shouting out hallelujahs in an unseen choir – all you get back is what you are worthy of – an echo, not an answer!

I was once warned about the possible dangers of repeatedly making use of an ouija board – and indeed that there may be long term consequences. Why? Should it really be any different in the spirit world, provided that we show consideration and deference; perhaps actually encountering a person sat in your rocking chair is the difference of the deference?

I never imagined that one day I would be blessed with the good luck of discovering Martha Amersley and her family. I learned so very little regarding especial events in Martha's life, but that's not to say I did not learn a considerable amount regarding Martha, particularly that she was always going to be there for me – she was like my spirit buddy! She always listened earnestly to my every word, but sometimes there would be a hesitant pause before she replied – as though she was mulling over what I had said. Although often after her contemplation she would reply with something less than spectacular – her reply was always unquestionably worth waiting for though.

Neither of us made any unrealistic demands – just two regular folk shooting the breeze together. When Martha could not recall some happening, she would say so without hesitation, and I never had any cause to disbelieve her.

Sometimes speaking to her could become a kind of conundrum for me though. For instance, imagine if I were speaking to Mom Brady (Brady Bunch) we would effortlessly identify with the trials and tribulation of everyday life in the 20th century – like raising children perhaps (they had six!) The Brady's were a regular American apple pie family – the Amersley's were colonial farmers in 1763 British North America!

Martha and me would chitchat relevant to the planting and rearing of corn, potatoes, turnips and such. Have heart to hearts over the aggressive growth of weeds in British North America and have in-depth debates over what to do about manure from the neighbours' stock lying uncollected in the woods!

I have no doubts that creating and running a 1763 colonial farm was no mean task, and dear Martha wanted to share that with me in every detail each time we became 'plugged in!' I guess the only similarity between the Brady's and the Amersley's was that they both had six children.

To try and sidestep the talk about planting taters and such, I intentionally asked Martha if she could recount a definable event in her life. She acquainted me with how the native Chipewyan Nation was devastated by smallpox in the 1780s!

How strange it is
to come across one of your
observations
and to find out I can now
accept
my own
21st century
diversity.

6

Ipsisima Verba ~ at bedtime!

BY THE TIME Molly had reached her early teenage years we had adopted a most raggedy senile German Shepherd dog named 'Bebop'. Molly set about tutoring him and such, but Bebop never really did get the hang of it!

We went through a routine where, in early evening after taking Bebop out for a pee, we'd return home, stoke up the fire and spend the remainder of the evening ridiculously cogitating over the lives of 'our' ghosts. We always referred to them as 'our' ghosts because it was us who had initially beckoned them in in the first place – unquestionably, it wasn't as though they came into our home uninvited.

I remember asking Molly once "I wonder how our ghosts looked long ago? Were they young, handsome, fragile, or special even – and how will they look in twenty-five or fifty years hence?"

Molly gazed fixedly into the coals in the hearth before giving me her reply and then unhurriedly said "Dad, there aren't '*consequences*' where they come from and so why should their ages be dissimilar to now?"

I remember how I thought that Molly's evaluation was so spot on. For example, the things that we lose in life, like perhaps our misplaced youth or maybe a lover, became the senseless irretrievable 'doodahs' that we tend to covet the most. However, our ghosts never mention such inconspicuous triflings – these things are of no special interest to them – in other words these things neither matter nor don't matter at all!

Like Sunday neighbours chatting knowledgeably away on the corner, Molly's astuteness and my pretentious wisdom were always as pure and as commonplace as the air we breathed!

Around the time when the coals began to collapse into the grate, our lust for secrets and opinions regarding the 'other side' had grown into purely a lust for our beds. Although unsure of their exact lines, our in-house occupiers would undoubtedly have the last word that evening, as they always do!

Footsteps on the bare floorboards in the old garret upstairs – humping and bumping across the carpeted lounge. A simple shadow that wasn't Bebop moving arduously down the stairs. Soothing natural phenomena, like the squalls of wind that rattle and rake at the loose window panes. There is sweet Fanny Adams to be alarmed at. They are merely night sounds on the very brink of brilliance that we have grown accustomed to and love.

I know only too well that they are in all probability watching over us with their oblique faces, and who am I to offend them? I am somehow afraid that if they go away I might miss them and indeed they may miss us as well. However, what words of sensibility are left when you are tired and want to sleep – so goodnight my incredible friends, goodnight!

I make words for people
I've never known
They are safer than
the ones I've known.

7

"You took the words right out of my mouth"

– Micky Spillane's *'Kiss Me Deadly'* –

RALPH MEEKER'S SNEER on whether he reads poetry or not, stiffened still by his brilliant Brilliantine brush cut, was enough to put even Christina Rossetti in a weir of whirling celluloid – she never figured on seeing the world on fire in any event! However, any way you cut it, the answer is always the same – in the liver, in the heart, in the house across the street, death is always very close indeed.

So sleep quietly dear Marx and Freud, for you are merely figureheads to our transition from life into death and nothing more! It is only when Jesus is finally arrested for being an imposter that you Marx and Freud can raise your brows and hand out your own high-minded views regarding the prospect of 'being dead.'

> *"On a hot summer night, would you offer your throat to the wolf with the red roses?"*

Poor wolfman, frazzled, spooked and all played out. He bit the hand that fed him once too often. I guess there's a little desire for death in everybody! Although the best study in jaded jugulars I have seen was our pet bat who would 'hang around' in the bathroom for me every single morning. He had this peculiar partiality for my shaving cream!

> *"Will he offer me his mouth, his teeth, his jaws, his hunger (x2) and will he starve without me...and does he love me?"*

Let's be clear – no animal eats its mate's throat – except perhaps insects when it's the protein they are after.

Alas that poor wolfman again. For him it's dogfood in the bowl. No one loves a fella with hair sprouting out all over and who runs around crouched on all fours sniffing the mulch of sodden leaves and stale piss under tree trunks.

There is nothing left of his once kindly smile, but yellow eyes and yellow teeth. However, he still has carte blanche to growl and tackle women over sixty carrying groceries!

I often fancied dressing in buckskin, not to be like a wolfman, that's too far out, more to be like Hoppy. I'd need a black Stetson as well though!

> *"On a hot summer night would you offer your throat to the wolf with the red roses?"*

NO!! Imagine Karloff handing you a business card with a complementary rose. I say let those angels of wrath alone. I don't like doggy noses and cold things touching my skin anyways – do you?

8

'Cosmic' objects

ONE DAY IF I wake in a beautiful clearing surrounded by angels with blue wings; transparent blue wings through which I can see into a beautiful overgrown garden of flowers and butterflies. If one day that happens, will a normal course of events follow or not?

Will I feel hunger or thirst? Will I experience warmth even though I am stone cold? Will I shed tears of happiness or dread when I am dead or merely despair? Will I still be able to acknowledge love, desire and heartbreak? Will I still cherish my friendships the same when I am dead or would eternity now be my only best friend and feigned companion? Will I be able to inhale and enjoy the fragrances of all of those flowers in the beautiful overgrown gardens?

How could I pretend that so-called end 'heaven' is completeness, when ostensibly without hunger, thirst, warmth and desire etc it would just simply be the end; period! But folk do!!

9

The sense of solitude

ONE RAINY DAY I'll climb the rickety stairs to the loft and liberate all of the rag dolls and cuddly creatures from the crates they've resided in since Molly grew up. There's almost certainly several hundred little memories tucked away up there and one rainy day I am going to find them all new homes in every nook and cranny of our home – they'll be like little bijou ornaments. Molly would like that!

Those rascally playmates of past times, stuffed with the sentimentalism of their reposed existence – perhaps nourishing one or two twilight moths, yet mindful of their worth to us, their family. Incapable of uttering a single word they gaze tolerantly in whispers of expectation through their eyes of glass and beaded dots, waiting and preparing for the prenatal noise of my footsteps on the stairs to the loft like awkward little animals, their hibernation has lasted long enough!

10

Time travel??

MOLLY AND I used to have some quite lengthy discussions regarding the source of our ghosts. We never really fed into the popular explanation that ghosts are the spirits of dead people appearing in visible form.

I'd been at work all day, collected Molly from the university and now it was around 7pm on a November evening. As we pulled up outside the old parsonage Molly glanced up at the second storey window. The lights were burning which meant that our unearthly friends were visiting. "They startled me for a minute Dad, I thought we had burglars." As we entered the hallway Molly hollered "You quit your stamping round up there – you sound like stud horses!"

The ashtrays still held last night's cigarette ends, the sofa pillows had not been straightened and there were several magazines on the floor in the exact position in which they had been left the previous day, and yet upstairs the beds were made, there were clean PJs folded on the pillows and the rugs had obviously seen a vacuum cleaner. It's strange how our attentive friends have such a limited partiality to house chores!

I flopped into the comfy Chesterfield. "Reckon you're gettin to be quite a gal for making coffee for your old Dad" I said. "How old're you now?" she cheekily replied, but made us one anyway!

"Have you ever considered that perhaps our visitors are in fact time travellers?" Molly asked. "I don't mean as we see it in movies, Doloreans, phone booths and such. Perhaps God himself is a time traveller?" Molly was really in full-blown discussion mode now! "Think about it Dad. God is a stammering non-extremist type of guy who is forever reiterating how he created this world just how we wanted it. Somewhat a large undertaking unless he had already known what was up ahead. Do you remember when I was small we would often receive a visit from a guy we named Father Mike – said he was our shepherd and protector?" Molly paused briefly as she slugged down her coffee, then continued.

"I always imagined him as being a long grey-haired person with beady eyes. However, the stories he's gathered on his travels could not have been plucked from one lifetime and the clarity of his stories was so crisp it was as though they had happened only yesterday – perhaps for him they did!" Just to add a little more spice, as Molly often did, "and then there's the *Mouberly-Jourdain* incident!"

Molly had an insatiable curiosity about events that cannot be explained by science or the laws of nature. When she was little she had been content to let books answer her questions, but now she tried to learn from people. She would ask questions of everyone whom she deemed would be the most enlightened, of these was her late Grandma and me!

"Have you ever considered parallel universes?" I asked her. Molly obviously had but I continued in any event. "What of *The Ghosts of Petit Trianon?*" I asked. "It's just another theory for ghosts that relies again upon the nature of time. For example, Einstein in formulating his concept of time and space pointed out that all everyday experience is within a four-dimensional frame and therefore past, present and future can co-exist in an infinity of parallel universes."

"Dammit Dad, what are you saying?" she sighed impatiently "that when someone 'sees' a ghost they are merely looking out from their own time-frame and observing events in another, but what if the so-called ghost is in their own time and we just happen to be visiting that time?"

"Either way it doesn't matter" I replied "because death has never happened to them, they are as non-imaginary as we are to them."

I think we were both beginning to become teed off with this conversation as Molly threw in a bunch of her very own super-natural superlatives.

"It seems to me" she began "that time travel per se is not pos-sible because there is only one 'now' and for time travel to exist, two or more 'nows' would need to exist simultaneously!" She was in full blown mode again. "If any 'now' in the past or future is available for us to travel to, then all 'nows' exist at the same time. Meaning time does not truly exist because everything is indeed happening at once. In other words, there is only one 'now', one present moment and no time at all!"

I just sat there dumbfounded and speechless as Molly picked up the ashtrays and coffee cups and beelined directly to the kitch-en, singing radiantly as she went

"Where did you come from, where did you go?
Where did you come from Cotton-Eye Joe?
Get out your fiddle; rosin-up your bow.
Play an old tune called Cotton-Eye Joe.
Where did you come from where did you go?
Where did you come from Cotton-Eye Joe?"

11

9/11

THE VERY BITTER lesson that anyone who likes to write has got to learn is that a thing may in itself be the finest piece of writing they have ever done, yet it has absolutely no place in the manuscript. That's why I've avoided using all types of overworked metaphors and alliterations and will continue to do so and that's why I've felt the need to hold back from revealing to you what form of outward appearance our 'visitors' materialise in; until I felt enough time had elapsed to gain your undivided curiosity!

In the early years, say back in the 1960s, it all began with a simple ouija board which my Mom had handed over to me after she found out I'd been using one of her fine Waterford tumblers. I guess that from that point onwards that ouija board opened the door to all kinds of goings on. It's difficu lt sometimes not to make our 'visitors' visits sound as though they are visits from dead people – when in fact there is every chance they aren't. For example, they come in every form, facet and guise imaginable – in other words they are no longer pointer moves around a table! These (for want of a better word) so called 'apparitions' are truly as distinct and clear as any regular person. For me, the only circumstances in which they really do spook a bit is when they tend to follow you around and you are unsure as to whether it's a stalker or a 'visitor'!

September 3/2001 – Molly and me arrived at JFK to celebrate Labor Day – it was something we did every year and always reserved a room at the Michelangelo on 51st Street in midtown Manhattan. Our bellboy Damon (and yes he lent a hand with our suitcases) explained how we could place our items for room service in the cavity of the hotel door – and abruptly he faded away through the wall – without a mandatory baksheesh! I'd thought it was kind of odd when he'd mentioned seeing mayor Jimmy Walker at the celebrations – my guess is that Damon was on The Taft's (Michelangelo superseded The Taft Hotel) payroll around 1926 – there was no other way to explain it or mayor Guiliani for that matter!

Molly had obviously given the whole scenario of events some careful thought and later in the day as we skim/glanced through the Guggenheim she quickly and unexpectedly piped in with her own very persuasive interpretation of the 'bellboy incident'.

"My perception Dad is that a person and place viz Damon and the hotel and including time and space are thoroughly interdependent on each other. They are one prerequisite of one another." She paused as I cut in "was he a ghost or time traveller then?" said I. "That's not the point Dad" she added – I think my comment may have needled her!

Molly was indubitably the most penetrating and deadpan conversationalist I have ever had the pleasure to tangle with, particularly and especially when she was a kid! I knew this head-to-head wasn't over yet!

Several days on we cried in unison with each other.

During the September 11 attacks of 2001, 2,977 victims were murdered. The immediate deaths included 265 on the four planes and 125 at the Pentagon.

Later that evening Molly penned this short epitaph:-

Who could have known that death's shadow was stalking…?

Weeping willows crying silent
Pines that cluster deep secluded
Oaks and ash like towering churches
Flog the innocent with birches

Hudson mists creep up and chill
Throughout the night of burning embers
Unknown arms reach unknown souls
Beyond the fear of wild September

Nesting deep within the copses
Praying to the wind in whispers
Suspended, floating in confusion
Drifting dead in dreamed illusion

Fantasy, emotions frozen
Bequeaths a hidden sanctuary
Resentments harbour deep within
Running into oblivion

Fasting brief in pain that spreads
Waking torment from our beds
Laughing as clowns – gritting defiance
Crying as infants – stepping like giants

We will remember you – we promise
Love's memory is evergreen
The beginning of the end is over
And it never deflected the American dream.

12

Home

OUR EVENTUAL BA flight back to the UK was a profoundly bittersweet one. It was as though we wanted to return home and yet somehow we felt compelled to stay.

Although when we finally drew up outside the parsonage I couldn't help but feel a certain sanctuarium of relief though.

It seems to me that the human mind is, with all its faults, a most fearful instrument of adaptation. In nothing is this more clearly shown than in the months and years that superseded the savagery of September 11. The human mind's mysterious powers of buoyant resilience and self-healing never fails to leave this writer at a complete loss for explanatory words. In an attempt to rationalise the events at all, in some kind of subliminal allegory, I would say we knew it was coming – it began in the Middle East three thousand years ago and ended in Manhattan! That's all.

Every time I return from a visit to North America I bring back with me an almost supernatural kind of Whitmanian energy – it clings to me like a resourceful residue.

Perhaps each of us are all of the sums of the people we have rubbed shoulders with and all of the enthralling localities we have visited – none more so than NY. Even though we are not necessarily 'counting', it is just a nakedness we enjoy that cannot be avoided.

Alas, on this singularly notable occasion I returned home wounded and I won't be well from any lack of trying any day soon. Not at least until the 'self-healing' I mentioned earlier kicks in!

13

Big arse!

IT WAS STILL the first of three exceptionally long wet days when undoubtedly the best place in the world to be is home. Every now and then I'd put my book down and meander across the room to gaze through the tiny leaded windows, anticipating that the rain may be relenting, but somehow it never did – just became more severe and intense. There was something almost transfixing watching the painted leaves swirling by and hurling themselves ungracefully onto the leaded glass; carried on by more from the ferocity of the wind sweeping across the river.

"What are you looking at Dad?" Molly apprehensively asked.

"Nothing sweetheart, just the storm" I replied positively.

"Don't worry Dad, things will get better, they always do" she suggested.

It was almost as though she knew what was really going through my head and so I didn't answer.

"Do you like bears?" I perked in. "Up in Northern Canada I once got chased by one when I was a nipper".

Molly looked at me sceptically. "What, a real life-sized bear?"

"Sure, a real life-sized one with a big arse" I replied "but I guess he wasn't completely in the mood to eat".

Molly sniggered! "You were too skinny a kid to be bothered with Dad".

It's strange how stormy, blustery weather can create an optimum in amongst emptiness and how that in turn can give a real lift to the conversation.

And now the coffee is perking and Molly is coming to me with biscuits and smiles – my overdue loan seems somewhat insignificant; and so it should!

14

"A kind of short person"

The Highwayman

The wind was a torrent of darkness
among the gusty trees
The moon was a ghostly galleon
tossed upon cloudy seas
The road was a ribbon of moonlight
over the purple moor
And the Highwayman came riding –
riding – riding
The Highwayman came riding,
up to the old inn-door

– Alfred Noyes –

Buses pass by our house sometimes but horsemen hardly at all

SID MARTIN WAS his name and he often came to visit us, usually when we were partaking coffee and cake just before bedtime. It was as though he was just passing through and, not unlike the highwayman in Noyes' verse, he didn't dally for too long.

Sid was without question the quintessential highwayman of folklore and with his features so handsome as to rival Mr Errol Flynn's Captain Blood. He even conversationalised with all of the fondant swash and buckle that old wives' tales are made by killjoys!

I particularly had a hankering for his 'immortalised' black silk shirts – so black they almost hurt your eyes. When, from time to time, he'd wing his arms around in expressive mode you could actually hear the wind current running through his full sleeves. Enough about shirts, but they were so unlike the tired black wash-ups that I buy.

Apparently highwaymen such as Sid thrived in England during the 17th and 18th centuries, almost becoming legendary and romantic figures. However we learned very little about Sid Martin, except that he was always rather animated about nothing we could recollect. He had a peculiar partiality toward coffee and cake and he was a kind of short person – perhaps 5' 2' in his thigh-high leather bootstrap boots.

When at such time he decided to bid us 'au revoir' it was not without the invariable riddle or some kind of preposterous conundrum. For example – "Why have all the wild roses withered on the moor?" – have they? Which brings to mind a very strand reflection he left us with several months ago.

Bearing in mind that we assumed that Sid is supposed to have arisen from out of the 17th or 18th centuries, then perhaps you will understand why I found his recent quote somewhat bizarre – viz: "did you know that neon is just as nice as afternoon sunshine?"

I shall put that summarisation on my enigmatic and dark list for sure!

The Highwayman
(an ode to reincarnation)

I was a highwayman. Along the coach roads I did ride
with sword and pistol by my side
Many a young maid lost her baubles to my trade
Many a soldier shed his lifeblood on my blade
The bastards hung me in the Spring of twenty-five
but I am still alive

I was a sailor. I was born upon the tide
and with the sea I did abide
I sailed a schooner round the Horn of Mexico
I went aloft and furled the mainsail in a blow
and when the yards broke off they said that I got killed
but I am living still

I was a dam builder. Across the river deep and wide
where steel and water did collide
A place called Boulder on the wild Colorado
I slipped and fell into the wet concrete below
They buried me in that great tomb that knows no sound
but I am still around. I'll always be around
and around and around and around...

I fly a starship across the Universe divide
and when I reach the other side
I'll find a place to rest my spirit if I can
Perhaps I may become a highwayman again
or I may simply be a single drop of rain
but I will remain
And I'll be back again and again and again and again

— Songwriter : *Jimmy Webb* —

In the song version each of the four verses was sung by a different performer.

First : *Nelson* as the highwayman
Then : *Kristofferson* as the sailor
Then : *Jennings* as the dam builder
And finally : *Cash* as the starship captain!

(also recorded by Jimmy Webb and Mark Knopfler).

15

'Mr' Cooper

APART FROM SID Martin there were many other luminaries who graced our hallowed portals. One was 'the' star and he always was 'the' star – namely, Gary Cooper.

Gary had already won immortality for me when years before I had watched him in the movie *The Virginian*. I went to see that movie a dozen times just to 'savour and delight' in the part where the baddy called Gary a "son of a bitch". The words kind of die on the baddy's lips as gun in hand Gary murmurs in that lazy drawl *"When you call me that; smile!"*

There were many celluloid western heroes who really didn't know a hackamore[1] from a cinch[2], however Gary positively was not one of them. He'd lived the life long before he played it on screen.

On one occasion when Gary decided to drop in and see us, my brother Mike was visiting us at the same time. Mike was kind of unthinking at times and lunged in to ask Gary what type of girls he liked? I thought it was a really invasive and impertinent question to ask, inasmuch that Gary was happily married in any event. However, Gary gave one of his 'savour and delight' replies: *"Really homely girls, girls with cross eyes, overweight girls. All shapes, all colourings!"*

It was a dazzling rejoinder to an absurd question from Mike. He was always so much more than just a performing personality. There was so much versatility, simplicity and balance even in his silence, and we were always honoured to see him.

---

[1] *Hackamore* – a bitless bridle on a horse
[2] *Cinch* – a saddle is secured by means of a cinch (strap)

16

As told by Molly and me

DAD SAYS THAT "all life is like the seasons of the year. It's set in a pattern, like time is, and each life follows its own pattern, from spring through winter, to spring again."

I'd never really thought about life in terms of the seasons in that way, but I remember when I was little I thought of life like the leaves on a tree. First there are little buds and then little green leaves and then huge big green leaves. In an Indian summer and fall the leaves stay bright and beautiful and then all of a sudden it's winter and they are dead and it's all over.

Winter had finally compromised to an unexpected ravishing spring and so it had become customary to take our breakfast out of doors under the antediluvian gazebo in the compound. We breakfasted on cinnamon and raisin bagels fresh out of the oven and cream cheese, dampened down with rich full-bodied coffee and there was early morning sunshine all over our yellow table-cloth and we were so happy.

"I've never lived any place longer than I've lived here" Molly said while chewing absentmindedly on her bagel and looking interestedly at the vivid patterns made by the hollyhocks against the wrought iron of the gazebo's frame.

"I never want to move away from here Dad". I smiled and I assured her that we wouldn't ever move away. "Maybe I will have to move away Dad if I decided to marry" she added, cross questioning me. It's all part of the whole stultifying stupid marriage pattern – that's what people do!

I took a glug of coffee and peeped over my bi-focals at her. "Perhaps you ought to become wed to one of our guests – they like it here too!!"

17
George VI and 'ANZAC'

WERE WE, MOLLY and me, primarily just inculcate subordinates who had become expected to enable access channels for those of the 'other side' who wished to communicate, or were we in truth willing and eager participants who had been drawn to the 'visitors' because they were and are aspects of ourselves that we have yet to experience?

I closed my eyes and leaned back into the sofa and let my thoughts drift, trying not to analyse or hook into the reason of it all.

I realised I was thinking too much. 'Just being' was perhaps the very nature of existence. I needed to relax into 'just being' before I could even attempt to identify what in essence our visitors were hankering for.

I breathed deeply and slowly surrendered until the feeling of 'just being' began to prevail, whilst at the same time I created a reality in my mind where no one should enter our home without our 'say so' like they had done several nights ago.

We had had a totally unexpected visit by King George VI (1936-1952). He didn't stay that long, but told us that "all men were equal" where he now was. You just never know who you are going to get – sometimes just fleetingly, other times they become regular visitors. Hopefully one person who was just passing through was Adolf Hitler! I asked him only one question "how was the war lost?" He wrote down on paper for me the letters ANZAC and then sort of slunk out.

I researched his declaration and seemingly 'ANZAC' are the initials of the Australian and New Zealand Army Corps. I think

Adolf was most likely referring to WWI – perhaps the central powers in Gallipoli?

18

Outward Bound

WE DRANK COCOA and played chequers and Molly beat me three games straight and then we went to bed. I sat on her eiderdown and we talked a while about Thoreau and Dickinson and how 'cool' it would be to receive a visit from either of them. "It's a shame 'we' can't decide who visits us Dad" she added silently.

"Incidentally I came across a new writer today in the college library" she perked.

"What, a real person or a 'visitor'?" I enquired.

"Not sure" she said. "He was a tall, handsome man with silvery hair, a slight moustache and smelled of Brussels sprouts."

"What was his name?" I asked.

"Mr Sutton Vane" she said.

"He's a visitor" I replied. "From England originally – not New England."

"I asked him about his books and he just replied – God's will to be done on earth as it is in heaven and then he walked out of the library."

Perhaps he wanted to make a statement to you Molly but chickened out? I'll get hold of a book of his tomorrow if the rain ever stops.

The story I told Molly:-

His story *Outward Bound* takes on the question of what happens when we die and who finally determines whether we go to heaven or hell!

Originally Sutton wrote the story as a play which became a novelisation and went on to become several movies. Here is a brief synopsis:

A diverse group of seven passengers, all strangers, meet in the lounge of an ocean liner and realise that they have no idea at all why they are all there, or where they liner is bound for.
Each of them eventually discovers that they are in fact dead and actually on a journey into the afterlife.

"Perhaps you and me are actually dead Dad" she raised the question in a kind of funky spooked way.

"We can't be" I assured her "otherwise your hair wouldn't have been ruined by the rain today!"

19

Immortal?

IT'S STRANGE HOW we often strive to escape from a reality which terrifies us and yet enjoy fictional DVDs and such accounts that are beset with dangers. I guess our grandfathers were relatively free of such jiggery pokery.

Nothing is like it seems anymore. Even journalists resurrect great figures of history, analyse their deeds and then with their vitriolic pens take pride and pleasure in presenting an epitaph of complete character assassination! Day after day we are fed the effects of a slow insidious poison – we have come to value the vulgar above the virtuous.

It seems to me that today we live in an incessant uproar of violence about violence and have become in danger of knowing 'almost nothing' about 'almost everything'! The 'un-event' has begun to be preferred to the event – there is no equilibrium to fiction v fact!

We still have our nostalgia of course, but even that is not so precious and kind as it used to be.

As so often happens our 'nostalgia' becomes blurred by the cobwebs in our heads and we tend to create myths and legends to suit the needs of our subjunctiveness. When what started out as fact is tottering on the brink of fantasy it almost develops a momentum of its own, startling even reality itself!

For today is the product of yesterday and tomorrow will be the product of today. No matter which way you look at it, history is now! Moreover, not only is every 'happening' a part of a previous event, it is ongoing, non-stop and constant. It may ripple over the ocean of larger events for years. Some may rebound, but always they will remind us that history is disturbingly recurrent.

Passers-by do still pass by our house. I've even seen some walkers pointing at it as though they had made a pilgrimage to see it. I guess most of us like to know what year we are living in, but living here at Hamptonia it was somewhat difficult to decide!

Alternatives…

Molly was playing with Bebop all over the lounge floor when she suddenly stopped dead in her tracks. She must have had a thought, I thought – and she did!

"Dad, there are alternatives" she said.
"To what?" I say.
"To living, a person can easily die."
"Ah" I say "but that's the easy way out, the hard way is to go on living!"
Molly looked seriously high-spirited "I have so much life and living that needs doing I'm surprised I never ever thought of death" she added. "I cannot imagine that alternatives exist for me – like they obviously have for our 'friends'."

I wonder at what point they became immortal, inasmuch that we started out with just receiving messages and now receive visitors that are as clear as regular folk? Has time run backwards for them or are they living past events in their own lives and in history?

20
Logical writing?

ALTHOUGH IT WAS an excellent idea, I never imagined that one day Molly would find it worthwhile to begin a detailed documentation of the unaccounted for 'goings-on' in our home. Evidently she had routinely made ad hoc entries into her own personal diary about some of the more bizarre events, but this new idea was, in journal form, a revealing and comprehensive narration of all every day phenomenon no matter how insignificant it seemed. Essentially it was also a storybook of our lives as well.

Molly told me she had an underlying need, perhaps a duty, to factually record our every day liaisons with our 'visitors' and to somehow apportion our experiences to the unsophisticated outer world. It's true, what we had become accustomed to, regular folk may find disturbing, but that was a risk worth pursuing, she said.

After a bit, when she eventually decided to show me some of what she had written, I have to admit that I was somewhat confused by her exclusively conversational style of writing. It was as though our 'visitors' were all 'talk'! Here, let me explain:

For English readers, I suppose the most curious thing about 'talk' is the writer's resolute avoidance of using the past tense. Not so with Molly however, because the past tense is for her the historic present! Howsoever vulgar this may sound, it's deterred my association with logical writing once and for all – enough said!

21

London Vacation

HERE IN THIS antediluvian house on the far side of time Molly and me were looking forward to our once a year break – fittingly linked to the festivities of Christmas. Traditionally we treated ourselves to a pre-Christmas break, essentially several days in London to enjoy the decorations and illuminations – especially Harrods and Hamleys; they were the top of Molly's myriad! Of course it wasn't purely the innovative window displays and such and, nonsensical as it may seem, our 'piece de resistance was the uniquely British phenomenon – the Christmas pantomime. It just seems to me that most British children are indoctrinated from an early age into the stylised joys of

"He's behind you" and "Oh no he's not" and "Oh yes he is"!

It must be the only place in this politically correct society of ours where all in sundry can boo, hiss and bellow at transvestites without being condemned for it!

When I was fresh under the collar I believed the hype that London was one of the best places to party in the world. Dependent upon your perspective I suppose in some respects it was. However, with my solid reputation as a 'club animal' I'd gotten to hear about a rather attractive piece of real estate in Ambrosden Avenue, SW1 that price wise was really going for a song. Seemingly the occupiers and the mortgagee were at loggerheads.

I lived there for a couple of years, but after I decided to move on I kept the flat as a nest egg for Molly. Now, decades later, it has become a perfect 'pied-a-terre' for Molly and me to snug down during our once a year happening. Still on the subject of our sizzling sixties studio flat, I must say my Molly has such a profoundly droll wickedness with her prepositional language. For example, when we arrived at the flat tonight she mentioned how the flat's décor made her feel like she'd walked into her old art history textbook!

We were both travel tired after the wearing train journey from Devon – that in mind, we swiftly picked up various victuals at Victoria Street M&S, hotfooted it home and settled down to watch an old video of The Twilight Zone.

I remember when it premiered on American TV in 1959 it wasn't long before even its very name became a part of our everyday lexicon, in fact just humming the iconic theme tune became a byword on anything that was in the slightest 'surreal'.

Molly and me must have watched every episode since she was about six years of age. She knew the Rod Serling introduction off by heart and could recite from memory every word in the same laborious tone as Rod.

Viz (reiterated by Molly):-

"There is a fifth dimension, beyond that which is known to man. It is a dimension as vast as space and as timeless as infinity."

"It is the middle ground between light and shadow, between science and superstition and it lies between the pit of man's fears and the summit of his knowledge."

She would pause here, just momentarily (unlike Rod) as though she was waiting for an audience to second-guess what was coming next:-

"This is the dimension of the imagination. It is an area we call The Twilight Zone."

I didn't really think there was that much between the ears of the elderly man with the suitcase who systematically perched himself upon the steps of Westminster Cathedral west doors – you know, the doors that open onto Victoria street. However, Molly had a different reasoning about the fella than me, in fact she had kind of taken to him, but in all honesty she did have a soft spot for lame dogs!

She said it was as though somehow there was a huge conflict going down between him and the Cathedral – gargoyles and all! "Current usage v established practices perhaps?" I supportedly added. "No, it's not that Dad" she cut in. "It seems to me that there are differences between what is permissible and what is expected from whatever standpoint you wish to interpret matters."

Perhaps the man with the suitcase and the steps to the west doors contained a similar introspective, inasmuch that there is hardly any divide between the earthly and the unearthly whichever you decide to plump for – allegory or parable, who knows?

All I can add is from a descriptive standpoint I thought the elderly fella had a face not unlike that of Saint Augustin – or Saint anyone for that matter! However, by the light over the steps he definitely had the eyes of Donald Duck! And what of the Cathedral itself? Looked to me like a sumptuous gigantic layer cake which, in all honesty, is how you might expect a Cathedral to look – isn't it?

Radiantly blushing and thick throated, Molly finally came alive enough one evening to speak to the fella. It began with him popping the question "Are you studying me? Am I nearer to whatever you speculated you wanted or expected?"

"The truth is I am uncertain whether or not you may be one of our 'friends'." Molly loosened up and added "I believe you may be, however there is something about you that is missing."

Perhaps her reply had been quizzically too multifarious. He peered back at her and for the first time he looked empty and totally alone. "Can the living reach the dead?" he half-heartedly asked.

"Yes!" Molly replied enthusiastically, and added "If they can't it's certainly not from any lack of trying."

He looked at her smilingly and said "You've tried haven't you?"

As if to bring some jest into the equation he noted "It seems to me you might have been a nun in your previous life – with your close-cropped pixie hair and all – a nun in love with God!"

The afternoon shadows were gathering as the day was beginning to go home. It was the in between time after the day and before the night proper. A cool wind was coming in off the Thames river, but Molly felt unsurprisingly warm. For what seemed like a prolonged silence, neither Molly nor the stranger spoke, until just when the silence was becoming monotonous he interjected:

"I make words for folks who will not hear, I give them tunes, I make rhymes and such for them yet they will not turn their faces to meet mine – they prefer not to know me. And what of me? I really don't need the companionship of these types. You and I Molly, it seems to me, that there are so many speeches that have been written for us – a kind of common language that tells us what words of sensibility we desire."

He looked straight at her in a serene yet resolute way "Are you familiar with the term Glossolalia Molly?" he inquired pryingly.

"Yes" she replied. "It's speaking in tongues and is extremely gibberish to listen to."

"You are smarter than that Molly, tell me more" he said vehemently.

Molly didn't need too much persuasion. Once she got on her soapbox there was no holding her back!

"It is believed to be a 'direct line' to the throne room and thereby actually talking to God. A kind of supernatural outpouring for those who believe."

"Wow girl" he intercepted. "Impressive! It's the prayer language of the Pentecostal churches as well Molly. A person who has what is known as 'the gift of tongues' is usually themselves in the midst of religious ecstasy, trance or delirium. The speaker and often witnesses too believe they are possessed by a supernatural spirit and are channelling the language of this divine being – although all of the words are incomprehensible!"

"It's a helluva thing for a pretty young girl like you to be thinking about Molly, but it's been a real pleasure meeting you."

She glanced up at the second storey windows of their flat. The lights were burning which meant that Dad was home and she should be home too!

* * *

The most wonderful boho French café this side of the Channel is Maison Bertaux, where the surroundings appear as if they'll crumble to the touch, just like their exquisite cakes. Molly and me drowned each other with intoxicating articulation – a quality martini and excellent wine!

We missed our 'friends'. It seems that after several days away from them every infinitesimal minute was wasted.

"Perhaps we could grow wings and fly back right now" Molly suggested as she twilled her finger around the rim of her wine glass in a monotonous gesture.

"Do you remember that old girlfriend of yours Dad, Dr Ingrid Proulx, she was a nuclear physicist or some such? Didn't she teach at The University of London? I remember she bugged you into doing a talk to a bunch of her students and then you and her never dated again."

"I'd had a few martinis that day Molly and decided to give her students the benefit of my theory of 'threes'!"

"Apparently I'd stated that I'd been able to reduce nearly all of my life and the things around me into 'threes'. And for better or for worse I had always had a strong belief in the 'three syndrome'. For example, whether one was speaking of morning, afternoon or evening; the Blessed Trinity; birth, life and death; or true art, which in order to have a permanent impact must indeed have a beginning, a middle and an end. In fact, art to be art has to have a premise, a destination and an in-between vehicle for travelling there! My novels for instance are made up in part by 'three' trilogies and 'three' individual novels."

"I remember finishing up on a light note about how I perceived my life, inasmuch that it was now entering its 'third' stage – the stage that I consider to be the most productive seeing that all three of my wives have come and gone. When you think about it Molly, those marriages had no choice but to come and go inasmuch that they had such obvious distinctions from each other and, for that reason, the third divorce is really only a logical extension of the first and/or it is totally different, but could not have started or ended without the previous periods that had gone before it."

Molly looked at me mystified. "Dad, if in your mind there is some dark corner not yet occupied with numbers, then you might need to go right on 'a-preachin', but Dad, none of it makes too much sense to me in any event!"

22

Esther & Abraham

IT MAY BE a brutally effective characterisation of humankind, but nevertheless it undoubtedly brings to the fore and emphasises the sheer horror of either voluntarily or unintentionally involving outsider or newcomers into our realm of consciousness; whatever the appearance of verisimilitude it is open to fault finding by mockery at best!

Although there are probably countless dilettantes around the country who systematically dabble in the inappropriately named 'hereafter', our cautious probes indicate that numerous are rather benighted not only in their cultural understanding and moreover simply primitive in their imbalanced identical notions.

Take for instance the somewhat 'major-domo' in our unassuming household, viz Martha Amersley. This shrewd, sharp-witted entrepreneur who is raising her family in earliest America has the wherewithal to triumph in any period of yesteryear.

When you have a conversation with Martha there is a kind of weird electric feeling that runs through your bones. The only way to describe it is that it is similar to when you are first in love. A kind of omnipotence – a madness and anticipation to hear what zeitgeist mood and period in her life that she is going to familiarise and involve you in. It seems to me that anyone paying attention within say a twenty foot range would be aware and in total reverence of her simplistic intelligibility and unpretentiousness.

The shadowed afternoon is moving into night now. I close the bedroom door behind me and hurry expectantly down the stairs. Who will I sit across the room from watching – my favourite poet, a movie star or merely some undiscovered and alone regular person?

Most certainly not – not on your life – will our 'friends' be up for discussion by others. The only mooted point for me at the present time is that I would like to entrust our tucked away confidence to another person's care on the understanding that they will keep it a secret, a special person that is.

I light one candle with another's flame. Coming back up the stairs to bed I start to approach the large chamfer cut mirror. I stop fleetingly and see just me in my loose-fitting striped pyjamas looking somewhat anachronistic in the chestnut coloured candlelight. Was I ever strikingly handsome, ever at all young and dishy, ever tantalisingly wise? My frown attacks my reflection head on here in the harsh candlelight of solitude – even a funhouse mirror would be more compassionate – of that I am sure.

I pass my Molly's bedroom and look across at her curled up and sleeping. Bebop, forever her intimate, laying by her side just blinks at me in bare consciousness.

Before I catch my stalking silhouette against the wall, I finally reach my own bedroom. Safe. I hit third base and slide to home beneath the covers.

Damned lights had fused again, short circuited, stopped working, blown abruptly and unfairly – proceeding en route to the bathroom. Bladder deficiency is no laughing matter as you become older!

Esther and Abraham are friends of Molly and me – yes indeed they are! They are the most intelligent, gifted and unaffected couple I know. They had worked for the financial service firm Cantor Fitzgerald who occupied the 101st to 105th floors of the north tower in the World Trade Centre. But for a twist of fate on that disastrous Tuesday morning, I may have lost them.

They came to stay with Molly and me for a while after 9/11 and I got them through so many nights, but hey, that's what friends are for after all.

When we were young marrieds, I was with my first wife then, we all even experimented in sex together. When Molly was an adolescent teenager she taught their two children how to dive and swim and several years ago when we all vacationed in Canada I showed them how to steer a sled around rocks and boulders on a ground covered with too thin snow.

I had invited them to come visit that very afternoon and knew only too well that if there was anyone I should entrust with our protected secret it was undoubtedly Esther and Abraham. It seemed to me as well that Molly and me had carried the responsibility on our shoulders for far too long, like it was our 'duty' or some such. In many respects I wanted to unburden and come clean about the whole sequester of events.

We had an hour or so to spare before E&A were expected; Molly suggested that me and her should 'audition' each other in a similar way to which we would broach the subject with E&A. I agreed, my concern was that they both may have grown too 'homey' of late, and I didn't want to shock them to bits! I need not have worried because when our splendiferous buddies finally arrived it was as though the years had melted and that it was only yesterday we chewed the fat together.

In this second week of December the dark winter nights still had a long time to stay. After dinner that evening Abraham held court telling us stories belonging to earlier days – most of which we knew, but who's counting? Abraham had this photographic memory and he seemed to have developed a capacity for booze that could have retired him with the title! Stretching out stories, but not hardly getting to the point, was a speciality that Abraham excelled at. Esther had presented my Molly with some delicious brownies she had baked herself. Bright eyed and munching, Molly declared that she had reached her nirvana – clearly Esther had included her own distinctive ingredients to those brownies!

When Abraham paused for breath and a top-up, I deduced that this would be an appropriate opportunity to leap in with my Bill Blatty experience.

Remember William Blatty? He went on to write The Exorcist. I originally met him through his second wife, Elizabeth, during the early 1960s. He was older than me and he was one of the few men that I kind of respected. Him and me would often have long discussions (after Elizabeth had retired to bed with a headache!) about the true nature of good and evil; whether indeed spirits existed and whether the polarity in the universe was harmonious.

From time to time we used to have seances and ouija board soirees. It became a real social gathering. Bill would invite the whole gang; cronies, neighbours and anyone who was worshipping inclined. Apparently, or so I was told, Bill's idea for The Exorcist was born during these assembles.

The last time I saw Bill Blatty was during my brief visit to NY – we had a nightcap together and he considerately gave me a signed copy of his book.

His lack of concern was ostensibly so, when he sneered at the mishaps that had occurred on the film set. "Maybe the spirits are controlling the film, who knows?" he chuntered with a grin.

The time for secrets had arrived at last. Just let me end it, just let me begin it I thought frivolously.

"I shall now present the sneaky surprise of the evening" I commenced. Molly had been watching me stone faced. She knew I was struggling with the task before me. She knew that if ever an intervention was necessary, that necessity was now. When she cut in on my sorrowful effort I felt a gush of liberating relief run through my excusable soul.

Molly launched into it without fear or contradiction.

"Remember years ago when you and my Dad used to amuse and entertain yourselves with that home-made ouija board and how elated you all would become when it began to notch up all kinds of paraphernalia for you? Yea, I've heard all the stories and it seems to be that you all were pretty wrapped up in it. Well things have moved up a mite; perhaps you could call it evolution" she added, with a promise of the wryest smile.

"Nowadays, ridiculously real and regular folks not only visit us, they live with us in pure physical form. They, for all one knows, are passed away, however their presence in this house and around us generally is unaffected by their so-called death."

The room was quiet. We were all waiting for Molly to continue.

"I believe that the fundamental reason for them being here with us is because of the struggle some of them have to justify and preserve their thoughts within the limits of their supplementary existence. That is, somewhere within the original and the authentic limits. It just means that the struggle for unity between that existence and that which they call for (and possibly awaits) on the 'other side' is flawed. If not, then why do all of our senses propel us (and them) to find out more? Is it because we are each of us an intrinsic part of the self-same plan?"

After Molly's 'esteemed' performance I had a sneaking suspicion we were all temporarily incapable of uttering a single syllable. However, the speechlessness was broken by Esther expressing a wish to meet a guest caller. "You are an eloquent and persuasive speaker Molly. Perhaps they may require some coaxing?" she added in a kind of a whisper.

"We don't need to persuade or coax them Esther, they just arrive" Molly chortled. All of a sudden everyone wanted to have their halfpenny's worth, it was like a pestilence of questions from a clairvoyant proletariat who all knew the answers.

Abraham was looking for the last word which he was finding difficult to get in. Almost in a gesture of outworn anxiety he, without careful thought, blurted out "moment ago I was filled with the firm conviction that whatever is loitering out there can stay out there and now, moments later, I am so excited and restless at the prospect of meeting one or more of your 'friends'. Invite or invoke them Molly, please!"

She was very gregarious and outgoing. Having said that, there was much to be taken by her rather droll sense of humour. It seems to me that Southern ladies demand attentive listening. What with all of that slow Southern talk and the long pauses and its often dignified and almost cadenced rhythms.

All of her hyperactivity was targeted directly at Abraham. "I didn't recognise you at first" she laughed. "I was wondering if it really was you – the cunt who was trying to get near to me, but now doesn't want to know me!"

Now I know that memory does strange things to people and the passage of time since she was supposed to have 'met' Abraham probably amounted to around ten years, but Abraham seemed to me to be faultlessly knocked sideways in his tracks as to who on earth this woman was.

Esther, on the other hand, had begun to sound like a hacked off phonograph needle. "Who is she Abraham, who is she?"

Still the accusations of overfamiliarity stepped up. In a trilling, quavering tone she carried on. "Ok, I admit it, I'm pissed off. When we lay by the creek you led me to believe that you would be at the carnival yesterday morning and you never showed up! I've kept my distance trying hard to keep to the rules, but I have questions you need to answer or you'll regret it. Maybe not today or tomorrow, but for the rest of your life. Your excuse that you are married wasn't good enough in the aftermath!"

Outside the night sky was black. There was no moon. Our uproarious visitor reflected that there would not have been room for one, for all the available sky space was taken up with stars. She looked up at us all, breathed deeply of the warm scented June air...

To See Him Again

by Gabriela Mistral from "Poems of Love" dedicated to death

Never, never again?
Not on nights filled with quivering stars,
or during dawn's maiden brightness
or afternoons of sacrifice?

Or at the edge of a pale path
that encircles the farmlands,
or upon the rim of a trembling fountain,
whitened by a shimmering moon?

Or beneath the forest's
luxuriant, raveled tresses
where, calling his name,
I was overtaken by the night?
Not in the grotto that returns
the echo of my cry?

Oh no. To see him again –
It would not matter where –
in heaven's deadwater
or inside the boiling vortex,
under serene moons or in bloodless
fright!

To be with him...
every springtime and winter,
united in one anguished knot
around his bloody neck!

And left the room – it was like suddenly all of her accusatory depressions were gone.

I looked around at my somewhat dumbfounded group and remarked "Good-lookin' woman like that, you'd think she'd look to get married". Molly added "Perhaps she is the casualty of a terrible consequence to a marriage she once had. Perhaps she's still grieving for her husband; some widows grieve their whole lives long."

The Kingdom of death being heaven?

That night was one of sleepless indecision for Molly. However by the next morning there was only one answer and she knew it.

"Now ain't that a helluva thing?" Abraham laughed as he finished his coffee. I have never partnered a spook to a carnival – good golly Miss Molly!" The first meal of the day was a perfect time to clue everybody in to Molly's plan.

The county carnival and fair was an annual event and not for the faint-hearted. It was considerable in size and took into account side shows, rides and during the evening an amazing hoedown rumble in the old market place.

I guess we had all come to realise that our Southern belle was not hardly the offensive slattern she professed to be. If there was one thing that we had learned about our ethereal 'friends' was that the myth that death would somehow mute life's misfortunes was factually untrue – in fact death was simply a procrastination of what life had deferred.

On the evening of carnival day the empty fields that adjoined our home were besieged with just about everybody in town. There was a beautiful shoving, laughing, raucous crowd that were determined to have a good time or die tryin'.

Molly adored the Ferris wheel. From the ground it was impossible to see the top seats. The bright lights which decorated the sides of the wheel were visible only through the mist coming in from the sea so that it looked as though the people in their seats at the top were disappearing into another world as the wheel spun slowly. It reminded Molly of the movie *Outward Bound*.

Abraham and 'Scarlet' moved toward the bop of the music – we tagged her Scarlet because of her Southern dialect!

"How could he ever have said that he loved me and wanted to marry me?" she asked Abraham. "How could he have loved me and then passed away into oblivion like he did? Would you have done that Abraham?"

Abraham replied. "Perhaps the truth is too disagreeable to be faced dear Scarlet. Perhaps it was you who passed into oblivion and he was unable to follow!"

She gazed at folks dancing like pricked balloons all over the floor and a curious sadness bled across her face. Recklessly, almost startling herself by the movement, she grabbed Abraham's hand and twirled afloat onto the dance floor. They both laughed happily, it was as though the tear of heartbreak that had hung so perilously on the fringe of her lashes had finally disappeared.

Scarlet would still visit us from time to time. We never asked her genuine name or indeed that of her wayward beau. She would usually take a seat by the window that overlooked the unkempt meadows waiting for her Johnny to come marching home perhaps?

23

The Priest

ESTHER AND ABRAHAM didn't require much of a nudge to stretch out their holiday 'stop by' because of "extenuating unforeseen events!" For the sake of elucidating, they were both becoming real fond of all of our 'visitants', not only but also inasmuch as the laid back way in which they looked in on us so willy-nilly, it was very endearing. "It's like we are in a new exhilarating situation almost every day" Esther observed (with zing in her voice!)

> And if we must look for heaven
> then heaven must surely be
> in arms that are warm
> and smiles if they tender be.
>
> *Rod McKuen* – extract from *'The Summertime of Days'*

Many happy encounters were to follow and once a struggling catholic Esther accepted the suggestion that perhaps she could kind of make amends with the Church by confiding and entrusting our secret to the parish priest. After all that is what priests were for, wasn't it?

The meeting at least with this particular priest was a disaster. All the good priest could proffer was "Let's hope that you will find solace in your long marriage and your good friends." In other words he implied that she was unbalanced – inappropriate for a priest to say...barking mad!

It is not known whether the sarcasm in her thanking him for having been a great comfort was detected by the good father or indeed whether he actually was able to foresee that to be the final scene of her attempted reconciliation with the Church!

Molly had often thought how nice it would be if her mother pronounced herself one evening, suddenly out of the blue. At nine o'clock that night Molly, clad in pyjamas and robe and ready for bed, was preoccupied in deep serious thought. Unfathomably deep.

She put her book down on the living room coffee table and her eyes fell arcanely upon the framed photograph of her mother. She stood still for a moment studying the dulcet face that smiled into hers.

"She was beautiful wasn't she?" Molly asked softly.

"Who dear?" asked Esther looking up from the account books she'd been completing.

"My mother" said Molly.

"Oh" said Esther. "Yes dear, yes she was."

Molly was still looking at the photograph. "She looks just like a princess" she said.

"What did you say dear?"

"Nothing Esther. Good night!"

"Goodnight dear!"

Molly lay in her wide four-poster bed and stared up at the cracked ceiling where the porch light outside made weird shadow figures with the room's darkness. Just like a princess she thought and felt a sudden tightness in her throat.

For a moment she wondered what her life might have been like if it had been her father who had died and her mother who had lived. At once she sank her teeth into the edge of the bed sheet in shame at this disloyal thought.

"Mother! Mother!" She said the strange word over and over to herself, but the sound of it in her mind meant nothing to her.

She thought of the photograph on the coffee table downstairs. My princess, she said to herself and immediately the image in her mind seemed to take on life, to breathe and to smile kindly at her.

Drained, Molly fell asleep.

24

Lynne

VERY EARLY THE following morning Molly arose and, unable to sleep, she was determined to make the absolute most of this irresolute yet stunning latish autumn.

She slipped quietly into her quirky psychedelic parka and with Bebop raggle-taggling along they bustled out toward the old spinney.

The sun had not yet risen and the autumn air was colourless and cold. Milky ribbons of sea mist still clung to the damp earth and the feisty sky was silver grey. The dirt path led to the woods past a bluff which commanded a sweeping view of the bay. The woods were in full autumn colour and scattered among the blackish green of the pine trees there were blunt exorbitant splashes of crimson and yellow.

Although Bebop was bounding about and sprinkling wee all over the map, Milly was full of wishful thinking and walked slowly along the leafy path. Now and then she stopped altogether and stood perfectly still, in the attitude of one who listens to a call from a long distance. Loitering and stopping in this way they reached the woods proper just as the sun arrived in haste.

Incredibly in the woods it was still almost dark and even the musical birdsong down the dirt path had been snuffled out. The air was close, quite warm and sour-sweet.

"Why, whatever brings you here at this time of the morning?" It was Father Humphry with his pint-sized pooch. She did not answer at once, but gathered the collar of her coat up close around her neck with a nervous laugh. When at last she spoke her voice had a kind of wooden tone. She wasn't altogether happy with the good Father's handling of Esther's query; too dismissive she thought.

Father Humphry looked at her in a knowing way. "Did you hear about the thirteen year old girl who fell from the bell tower and broke her neck? It was last autumn. I was sweeping up the leaves at the time. You know she didn't even cry out!"

"Yes Father, I had heard" she replied in a voice of controlled exasperation. "Nell in the Post Office has told me every terrible detail more than once" Molly added.

"Does it make you nervous?"

"Extremely, but not at all troubled."

She could tell from the good Father's expression that he was happy with her reply.

"Would you sit down for breakfast with me?" he added.

Through her mind passed a long panorama of plans which she had made during her sleepless night – tutoring French at the village hall, there was some sewing too that needed doing, lots of bits and bobs as well, but her intuition told her that nothing was quite so important as breakfast with Father Humphry that day.

The sun was brighter now and, as they came out of the woods, the sky had brightened into a flagrant warm brilliant blue. In the fresh air there was the odour of dung and burning leaves from Bob Butler's farm. Neither Molly nor the Father were that comfortable, perhaps a little apprehensive. They had been talking with grim vivacity about gardening as they yomped home, but now for one reason or another Milly figured that the tragic incident in the bell tower was silently significant to them both.

When Molly returned home later that morning, after having breakfast at the priory, it was with whopping passion and a buzz of edginess that I'd scarcely seen in her before. In fact I was getting as excited as she was and I didn't even know why!

"She visits him Dad!"

"Who?" I asked, at a loss!

"The young girl who fell from the bell tower, she visits Father Humphry frequently."

"Tribute to Father Humphry then" I mused reflectively. "That's probably the reason why he was unable to acknowledge Esther's divulgence as by doing so he would certainly have to admit his own secret which would have been disloyal to the girl."

"Peculiar isn't it Dad, how the clergy drum into their congregations all of the Litanies which have absolutely no bond with common speech until their own life begins to move precariously across the hills and down? I was unaware that this God could be such a complicated character!"

"By the by, Father Humphry cheerfully asked if he could bring 'Lynne' to visit us at Hamptonia. He remarked how it might help to give her an insightful understanding of the afterlife." I really cannot see how Father Humphry came to that conclusion, however I gave in quietly!

Neither the far away cry of love nor the nostalgic call of death disturbs anything inside me now

– Nichita Danilov –

During the next few nights Molly rested and slept quite normally. That night she had dreamed she was proprietor of a live-in linen shop. The outline was still very vivid in her mind when she awoke. She lay there and pondered pensively about how there was a kind of pleasantness in handling clean linen, especially qualitative items.

She sat on the edge of her divan and peered frowzily through the muck stained window glass. Dour storm clouds were gathering in the sky, but down near the horizon the heavens were still relatively clear and the sun shone down with gentle radiance.

She was trying to be somewhat philosophical about Father Humphry's proposed visit with little ghost girl Lynne, but had her reservations as to whether 'Hamptonia' was an ideal place for persons who might be undergoing an acute psychic crisis, although there never had been an atmosphere of death in the house. Even after Molly's Mom had died, the lives of all three of them didn't fragment or come to a close, it was as though the relationship was deliberately inclined to do the opposite – they became richer and closer.

The house itself irritated Molly a little, probably because of the haphazard and nonchalant way in which it had been obliged to be furnished in the past. There were too many bits and bobs of furniture – small pieces and quantities – that reflected the tastes and the preferences of three matrimonial homes. Along with overstuffed chairs, it kind of combined the aesthetic and austere with rickety apologetic chattels that could have emerged from MFI.

In the sitting room there was the conventional sofa covered with flower-patterned chintz, a couple of easy chairs, a rug of garish red and an antique secretary. The room itself had an air of flossiness that Molly abhorred. The lace curtains looked rather dingy and on the mantel piece there was a heterogeneous collection of framed photographs and ghastly gewgaws. There was no feminine impression made by the room as a whole and this further exasperated Molly!

The flood would never sweep our house away, for who'd be left to watch the sunset when we're gone?

Rod McKuen from *In Someone's Shadow*

25

Katharine

THE AFTERNOON WAS fine, sunny and cool. The early spring air was bracing, bitter sweet with the distinctive smell from the pines and sodden leaves. There was not one cloud to untidy the spacious blue sky and all seemed well in the world.

Katharine's horse 'Hamptonia' had not been exercised that day and seemed somewhat restive in his stall as she arrived for her usual afternoon canter – perhaps from the expectation of the sugar-coated candy she gave him! She had ridden Hamptonia only five times before and on each occasion he was apt to be hard to manage – hence the candy!

They had started at a slow gallop along the bridle path. The path led steadily but not steeply upwards with the woods on either side. Now they approached the bluff, a stunning panoramic tract from which you could see right across the whole expanse of the bay for miles.

Katharine was always struck by the wonder of the view and never grew tired of it. She had it in mind to pause for a moment and drew in her reins. At this point, without warning, Hamptonia swerved harshly to the right and plunged headlong down the side of the precipitous embankment.

There were many contradictory interpretations by both press and crazy individuals giving different accounts of Katharine's tragic death, even four so-called witnesses who were supposed to have seen the whole thing whilst picking bluebells in the woods!

As the reports continued to come in in verbal bunches, paragraphs of bilge and folded paper pushed through the letter box, I was seized, not so much by a sense of sad frustration, but as a feeling that there were now enough conflicting stories to enable me to experience my own private 'Rashomon'. How could I hope to unravel anything?

I remember her sat in the makeup chair trying to relax with her eyes closed allowing the makeup artist to do whatever he wanted to do with her face. She had been a star far too long and would do anything to be loved; not to mention being a homemaker. How could I hope to unravel anything but not at all?

There is nothing more I wanted, nothing more than the truth, so that I could bury her with it. What I was faced with was the unrealised potential of her life which she surely forfeited to be my wife.

Do not think me sorry for myself. I am not. I have, in fact, no sense of self. But I am looking.

It was the first of November – five months have passed since Katharine was taken.

The bluff escarpment – the feel of her frail body beneath the cloth of her 'redingote' – the pervasive scent of her perfume – all of our high-blown discussions and tender heart-to-hearts…

… I can endure anything except diversity and Katharine always knew that. On account of which is why she presently looks in on me, nightly.

26

The doll!

THE FIRST SNOWFALL came early in December. It was some surprise. We didn't normally get through so much snow in this relatively mild region. I still remember now how make-believe the world looked from our mullioned sitting-room window as I quickly dressed wimpishly behind the stove. Molly mentioned that the whole world was changed by just that one pasteing; the little pond was frozen under its stiff willow bushes and huge white flakes were whirling near and far – the distant green meadows had faded out into fake ghostliness.

The basement kitchen had been commandeered by one and all. It was safe, warm and seemed most heavenly. Central heating was not an affordable frill, so we all huddled around Mr Cast Iron Pot Belly and redeemed ourselves with strong tea and buttered crumpets.

Abraham and Esther had long decided to lengthen their so-called stopover, but in any event this change in the weather made sense to stay put a while. The truth of the matter is that Esther was forthright in revealing to me that "Abraham and me, we ain't goin' anywhere, not until we get to the bottom of this weird spooky business. You hooked us in and now we're immovable!"

I just smiled back at the pair of them, like they were ghosts too "you know you are very welcome to stay as long as you wish." Molly was chuckling in amusement at the rapport going on between us old friends and make-believed to bang her head in a humorous exasperating manner upon the kitchen table!

All of the old house was very quiet of late. It was almost as if it seemed to be gazing inward at us all and pondering upon its next move. Darkness had begun to gather all but fortuitously in and around the thick leaved undergrowth that thicketed around the kitchen basement yard, although the night time proper was not yet in the undecided sky.

"I think something is radically wrong with the spontaneity of our 'friends' recently" Molly retorted and then jocularly "I have a peculiar foreboding in my bones" she seemed to be on a 'nattering' role now. "I often wonder if our friends make big salaries. I mean do they receive any remuneration at all? Are we indeed saleable items?"

"How would I know?" replied Abraham with a rascally sour looking expression on his face. "Do you have a practical reason for asking Molly?" He guessed she probably did!

"Well" she paused briefly "earlier this very morning on the south staircase, which only leads to my bedroom, I came across a doll sitting kind of intuitively half way up the stairs looking expectantly for me to find it." Molly paused again for a few seconds which seemed more like a few minutes and then scrutinising everyone, one at a time, she continued "this wasn't just some auspicious doll from Primark, it was a seriously 'costing a bomb' doll! We had all of us fastened seriously upon Molly's every word now. It was a comparatively thickset doll with a large reddish face and light reddish-yellow colour hair. I didn't care for her bulbous china eyes that opened and closed with the slightest movement, and those yellow eyelashes. I put her in a lying down posture so that the eyes would remain shut – those eyes really freaked me out!

It was the coldest most bleakly uninspiring December I have ever known. Even customary sounds used to carry far away. Often when I let Bebop go out for his bedtime wee and his time-honoured howl into the night, I swear folks could have heard that howl in the village some three miles away. We kept fires going in any rooms that had hearths. Day and night it was all systems go!

We all liked to congregate in the kitchen. It was the snuggest muster point in the house and always felt very hospitable as well.

Molly had been rocking slightly in her chair – the way you do when something tizzy is on your mind. She was not sitting in a rocking chair per se. She had devised a method of tilting back in her straight chair then letting the front legs hit the floor with little taps – her right hand holding fast to the kitchen table's edge for balance! She stopped rocking herself when Esther began to speak. Molly thought highly of Esther and Esther felt like a valuable link to her mother. In fact Esther was as good as, or close to a resemblance of, her mother in many ways.

"I frequently think about the various folks I have known and lately I kind of wish that perhaps one of them would present themselves to us. My mother died on the very first day that I was born, so perhaps it would be injudicious to count her. I still have a photograph of her though in the bureau drawer at home – all folded up with the napkins! Then there was the first boy I ever went out with. His name was Michael Moore. His whole platoon was wiped out during the Vietnam War. We weren't told about the circumstances until years later. I watched the funeral procession from the sidewalk, but I was not invited to the actual funeral and I don't know why."

"A young black boy, name of Ebenezer Jones, used to run deliveries for my father's store – he just disappeared. The Klan were very, very active in those days and there was talk that he was murdered."

"And Mr Donald Sacks. I knew him well, often came to our house for a little light refreshment with my Dad. He climbed poles for the telephone company."

"ALL DEAD!"

"And in the worst possible occurrence we all lost Katharine – I would give my eyes to see her, either in this world or the next."

Esther reached in her apron pocket and found a pack of cigarettes and matches. She lit a cigarette and put her arms around
her knees. Just to mention Katharine made her feel like she was
so empty; there wasn't even a feeling or thought left in her.

27

Molly's story...

A SOMEWHAT PROFOUND change came over my Dad after Mom's unaccountable accident. He would oftentimes disappear for long ad hoc walks alone. On numerous occasions I'd be looking around the house for him only to discover he was off on one of his walks.

These tenacious rambles extended for miles in all sorts of directions that I imagine covered the gist of the village and the countryside that surrounded it and that he and Mom had at one time walked together.

Routinely he would be spoken to and would stop and chit-chat. Dad was never inhospitable. If indeed the person who spoke to him was a comparative stranger, he'd relish the opportunity to acquaint them with Mom and pull out of his pocketbook a publicity photograph of her. Perhaps so that his own reticence would likely be understood by them.

He came to be known rather endearingly among the traders and storekeepers in the village as 'the bloke who was married to that actress'.

Dad was kind of relieved to be stopped by folks who wished his company. After all he was only walking and not really heading any place in particular. From time to time I'd tag along beside him not knowing to this day whether or not it was the right thing to do. When he came across one of his cronies he would allude to me as 'Katharine's daughter'! He was so proud of me, but it was as if he felt all the compliments for my rearing ought to go to my Mom and that his contribution was inconsequential; which of course it wasn't. It was gratifying that I was 'Katharine's', but inconsistent with my love for them both.

His blue-green eyes seemed to take in everything around him. Every merciless recollection was just power for the course; although surprisingly in his face there was a remarkable look of peace. A look I would say that is seen most commonly in those who are very wise or very sorrowful! There was something acutely steadfast about the way in which he would always keep his hands stuffed down into his pockets, but whatever; it gave me the pleasant opportunity to link arms with his!

There were these expeditious rumours spreading around the village that, after Mom died, I had received a copious legacy in the Will and, by association, Dad had also benefitted! If only the delightful chatterboxes knew the truth they would be completely astonished and aghast. Truth be told, after the funeral was over Dad and me were broke (but not broken), browbeaten by the mortgagee's (but not beaten). However, isn't it an ostensible fact of life that often when someone close dies folk instinctively assume that the beneficiaries will clean up? They seize upon your finances as an explanation as to where you are now and where you are likely to be after the Will has been read. An explanation of us is quite frankly simple. We didn't have a nickel between us when Mom was with us and we have even less now!

What we did have was a point of reference and that in its way was our source of comfort viz: Esther and Abraham – most of the time, and Dad and me – all of the time. We had one another!

I showed Esther my short story and she suggested that I tag this funny furore as a dedication to my Mom – her friend:

By all accounts Esther and my Mom were, as kids, Salvation Army girls. Esther said they'd stand on any street corner in their red and blue bonnets and bravado, tinkling a bell as folks approached them in the hope that they may feel obliged to drop a coin into the pot beside them. Not many did and so they concocted another plan.

With the pittance that they'd earned they trotted off to the hardware store and purchased a long length of rope. "Katharine taught me how to turn it and in turn we chanted this naughty ditty in monotonous minor key voices":

"Salome was a dancer, she did the hoochie kootch
And when she did the hoochie kootch
She didn't wear very mooch!"

Esther put one hand on her head, the other on her hip and wiggled her bum.

"Salome is supposed to be more like a movie star Katharine" she laughed.

"I never imagined that one day Katharine would open at the London Palladium!"

"Yea I'll bet Esther – neither did Mom!"

28

The Homecoming

THE CHOPPY WAVES were gathering and rolling in, turbulently eye high and in yellowish brown multiples. Every tiny terraced cottage within the menace of the ocean's reach had fastidiously had its windows boarded up and carefully sandbagged the doors.

From the mezzanine balconies of the town council offices masses of confused seagulls were swooping and screaming inexplicably like Hitchcock hybrids. Whole families had either hunkered down like moles in their upper floor bedrooms, or were stopping over with family and/or friends on the higher points in town. I had heard on the early morning news that this somewhat unusual torrential storm was on its way across the Channel from Continental Europe – it's uncanny why foreign thunderclaps should sound more angry and menacing than British thunderclaps, but they really do!

Having come out on the bluffs for my usual early a.m. constitutional, all of this billowing and blowing had caught me by surprise, inasmuch that we don't normally experience storms of this severity. I can respectfully see the sea from the distance I am at and it's beginning to cut up really rough all at once. The young sapling trees we planted are waving 'good morning' at me with some gusto too and so stridently I make steps to Farmer Grey's barn in the valley to take shelter – it stands about half-way between our home, the town and bluffs.

In the meanwhile...

Molly is out of bed, showered and turns her attention to breakfast. She switches on the hotplate and sets the kitchen table up for the first lovely meal of the day. She has grown accustomed to me vanishing out onto the bluffs in the early a.m. of late and reasons I will be home in due course, so doesn't worry too much.

Esther has finished off their unpacking, put the clothes away in the closets and shoved their suitcases into the space under the beds – she has made up the beds and waits 'impatiently' for Abraham to shake a leg and get the 'heck' out of the bathroom!

Abraham double-checks his reflection in the multi-mirrored splashback to make certain he has made the most of his thinning hair over the proportional areas of his head that really matter – a highly qualified daily routine indeed!

And what of Bebop? He lays somewhat forlorn just inside the façade by the front entrance door – holding fast his pee, like a ruffled grouse awaiting its liberation!

The eternal magic of all eternal things. Things that can send dreamers out into storms and allow them the amazing ingenuity to somehow trace their way; 'a way' home again.

The eternal magic of all eternal things. Things that can once or twice make your dreams run into reality and make reality itself in the end dissolve utterly and completely into dream.

> *"Home is the sailor, home from the sea,*
> *And the hunter home from the hill"*

From *Robert Louis Stevenson's* '*Requiem*'

"Sure, it admittedly wasn't much of a day for a funeral Ricky Dale!" She gazed wistfully across the bales of hay and unswervingly into my eyes. "Even the flowers were dying" she added smiling saucily at me. "I just knew that the time would come when you'd finally rise up from infinity and come home to me Katharine, it was all just a matter of me keeping the faith in us and it would eventually happen. I had imagined that the likelihood of such an event would be in some heavy hidden middle night. Beyond doubt I never imagined that Farmer Grey's old barn would play such a significant role!"

"Did you ever assume that we'd meet again in the same unpolished manner as we met the first time Ricky? You, smiling a smile like Lewis Carroll's cat, me blue-jeaned and apple-cheeked. You, stampeding me back to your studio flat, me, just a frown or two away from thanking God you had a studio flat!"

"No woman could ever wait and wait for you the way I have waited Ricky. I have to hang around anticipating that you are in the same solitude before I could make my way to you; that's the way we all do things here."

We sat down together on one of the many soft bales of hay. The noise of the storm had either stopped or been blotted out from my awareness. Can the dead reach the living? I mulled the thought over and heard my head say 'yes'! From what Katharine says it's certainly not from any lack of trying either.

"Premeditation is the surest friend to me dear Katharine, I'd never have reached today unless I was always in total preparation and certainty that you would return to me – it was only those essentials that kept me alive"....Katharine interrupted me midsentence...."I dispute your last remark Ricky, you would have kept going even if I hadn't returned, you must, it is your duty because of Molly. She is our forever, at the end of now."

"Twenty minutes from now and Molly should have our coffee percolating. It's been 18 years less a week since I lost you, let me bring you home Katharine. Is it fair that you have slept through those eternal years while I was left wondering over why you were sleeping?"

She fixed her eyes on me, they were passive eyes and I knew the answer was on her lips. "Did you mention that our Molly will be serving coffee in twenty minutes Ricky? Then take me home!"

Through the near-deserted town we ambled leisurely. The clouds had indeed unlocked their fists and, although the rain poured down for a while, Mr Sun was not so far away that you'd lose hope.

Freely and Free we made our pilgrimage home; questions lingered as questions tend to do and I didn't really care or bet that I knew or wanted to know them – not either the questions or the answers!

29

Variation on a Theme

"So, SOMEONE ASKS this lady 'How's your lovely daughter?' 'Oh, she's fine and married to a doctor' says the lady. 'Wasn't she also married to a lawyer?' asks the first. 'That's right.' 'And wasn't she also married to a banker?' 'That's right!' 'Oy' says the first 'so much happiness from one daughter!'"

Molly doubled up with laughter, but Esther just sat there with a look of forbearance on her face – she'd listened to Abraham's Jewish showpieces many times!

There was an easiness being with Esther and Abraham seated at the kitchen table, even though Bebop was beginning to remonstrate – in spite of that, where was Dad?

Molly politely excused herself, hurriedly put on her top coat and, with Bebop close at heel, ran like lickety-split down the hill towards town. She was still running with a spate of hidden energy when she reached Union Square and heard her mother call out to her from the front door of the Thrifty Café. "Molly, Molly, Molly – we were just buying some hot baps for breakfast."

"Race you home Mom" Molly said as if the past years had been but a reverie. Katharine hurried to her side and they scooted off leaving Ricky to follow behind with Bebop.

Ricky had always been a firm believer in hunches – perhaps call them psychic foresight – and he liked to discuss his hunches with anyone who had a fervent interest in same. Ricky had hunches about himself, hunches about other people and hunches about the fate of the world. Indeed, many of them were actually confirmed by events! As he rounded the corner to the galley cookhouse he could make out uproarious heart-warming merriment from all and sundry at home and with a look of contentedness he cogitated "nay, I didn't see this heady hunch approaching!"

He had pursued a few women since Katharine's 'death'. Some young, sometimes beautiful and oftentimes in 'disrepair'. They were mostly disappointing encounters because his romantic imagination and true love were still involved with only one great passion – Katharine!

Once, long ago he had unwittingly upset her over some idiotic disagreement. He remembered seeing a flash of unhappiness on her mouth, so brief that only he who loved her would have noticed. He pretended not to have seen and yet his fingers trembled so violently afterwards that it took three matches to light his cigarette!

In the last spring of 1969 Dwight Eisenhower died, Neil Armstrong walked on the moon and Richard Burton gave Liz Taylor a million-dollar diamond nearly as bit as a cue ball; and Katharine cried at the end of every song in the church at Molly's baptism, memory is a strange phenomena is it not?

30

"61 rounds ridiculous! Worse than a fairytale ... or not?"

AT ABOUT FOUR o'clock in the p.m. an unusual 'visitor' unexpectedly appeared in our living room. We were all just sat around talking through the events of the past twenty-four hours and didn't really pay that much attention to him, or him us for that matter.

Straight away he spotted our splendid rocking chair in the snug inglenook and almost instinctively made a beeline to it. He made it his own and sat still, passive and relaxed with his powerful woolly head resting in neediness against the back of the wooden rocker and his brawny hands calm upon the arms. It came to pass that this enormous great black fella went by the name of Peter Jackson and, personally speaking, he was not a person who you would want to mess with!

He said almost nothing excepting his name and such the entire evening and smiled quite rarely, but as he rested there we all had this sense of his utter contentment.

Molly sympathetically fetched him a large tumbler of her home-brewed apple brandy "after your walk in the cold" she said.

His face had a look of weariness and pleasure, similar to that of sick people when they finally feel relief from pain. As he began to speak it was as though a faint flush came up in his cheeks. "I socked them damn hard" he began "four coppers in a row; I never wished to be troublesome to them coppers, but they went for me and so I socked them!" He continued "The last copper gets up twice on me, so I hit him with my left hand – I pack a very good punch with my left hand."

We persuaded our guest to stay and have supper with us; he needed little urging! As we all sat down together at the dinner table he smiled almost uncontrollably. It occurred to me that he liked the looks of us.

At nine o'clock in the p.m. precisely he quietly roused himself up and out of his chair and put back on his coney fur top coat and fur cap. After shaking hands and thanking us he turned to Molly and said meaningfully "you a good girl". Peter Jackson disappeared out into the night and I volunteered 'subserviently' to wash the dishes!

I called in at our local library the following day. I just had this niggly hunch that our 'niche' visitor may possibly have been a prize fighter and by all accounts my hunch was correct!

The story goes that in 1891 the great Australian black heavyweight got his chance to fight heavyweight champion 'Gentleman' Jim Corbett. After beating the living daylights out of one another for '61 rounds' the referee stepped into the middle of the ring and called out "I declare this 'no contest' as neither Corbett or Jackson is able to continue – all bets are off!!"

In the beginning Jackson had accepted to fight the great champion John L Sullivan, however, Sullivan proclaimed 'I am a Southerner, I will not fight a negro – I never have and never will!"

I would be fascinated to hear Sullivan's justification for that comment, but who knows, he may oblige us with a visit before long!

I decided to mention this kind of ambiguous comment to our Esther who was indeed raised in Louisiana. She installed a new slant on the matter for me. "Coming as I do from Louisiana, I know only too well that coloured folk are a lot happier in the South than in the North" she said. "They're appreciated as individuals in the South, although I must admit they're considered as inferior, whereas folks in the North pay lip service to the principle of racial equality, but scorn coloured folk as individuals!"

The straitjackets of race prejudice and discrimination do not wear only Southern labels. The subtle psychological technique of the North has approached in its ugliness and victimization of the Negro the outright terror and open brutality of the South.

– The words of Dr King –

31
Marriage and that confounded doll!

MOLLY RELAXED HER weary self against the puffy cushions on the Chesterfield with a contented sigh. She was relieved that she didn't have to walk Bebop this evening on account that Katharine and Esther had promised to do it for her.

It was a nice change to have an inkling of leisure time just before going to bed instead of 'charging' off into the night with Bebop. A little pampering time she surmised as she rubbed Katharine's Elizabeth Arden cold cream with firm, upward motions into her throat – just as she had learned from an Illustrated Woman's magazine article!

"Do you think it would be a good idea if Ricky and me get ourselves married again Molly?" This was a question from Katharine that Molly hadn't really given much thought to. Although it was perfectly acceptable for a widower to remarry, it was nevertheless understandable for the deceased not to be too overjoyed at the prospect of her husband remarrying. However, in this instance, it was seriously inconceivable that the deceased would want her husband to do anything other than mourn her departure for the rest of his life and for him to do that 'grave' requirement he needs to wed her!

Immediately Molly's common sense kicked in and confirmed it was entirely natural that her Mom and Dad should be considering their marriage again. Her emotions kicked in almost simultaneously as her common sense and giggling in heartfelt sincerity Molly replied "Congratulations, I think you will make the handsomest and most divine couple, dead and alive!"

Molly mentioned later on that she had seen a movie where the 'soon to be deceased' mentions to the 'soon to be widower' that it would be 'fair and decent' if he were to remarry. Molly, methinks that movie is 'strictly for the birds'!

Almost as soon as the 'bans' went up at the village church the scampish gossip regarding 'Ricky is marrying a much younger woman' was all around and about. Like a candy bar in the hands of children, it was not allowed to be shared overlong on one pair of lips before being passed quickly to another. There was also some observational prattle about how much Ricky's latest wife resembled his first wife – that gave us all an inwardly chuckle to say the least.

I know that Molly and I saw eye to eye on the institution of matrimony, although she had avoided it thus for herself. Indeed, she adored the miraculousness of newborns, not necessarily the hullabaloo of same though!

Perhaps, stemming from an early age, she was absolutely mad for dolls, especially when they began to devise dolls in diapers that peed and that you could change. She learned to walk pretty quickly by pushing a toy carriage around the house with a doll in it too!

My greatest pleasure was watching her pushing a doll buggy through Cary Park, noisily playing Mommy at the same time. She wouldn't want to speak to other little girls if they didn't have babies of their own.

Once an elderly lady asked Molly who her baby's daddy was? She replied without hesitation "Roy Orbison!" Katharine always dressed Molly in expensive and unusual clothes (this was prior to us becoming 'have nots') and from time to time Katharine would even make matching outfits for those dolls – and there were many!

Molly's gran sternly told us that we ought to dress our child like other little girls, and if we didn't we'd have a problem on our hands – we didn't and on the absolute contrary Molly wasn't!

Now, where is this all leading to? With auspicious regard to that obtrusive doll that Molly came across on the stairs to her bedroom and moreover how it came to be there?

The somewhat strange occurrence reminded me of nothing I had ideas about or had ever heard of before and Molly left no doubts in the telling that it had freaked her out from beginning to end. She did add afterwards that it was kind of flattering and also rather intriguing (as far as it goes!) that someone had imagined this scenario of events especially for her. Summing up Molly said "It makes no sense, so I hesitate before I say it was a wonderful thought and, in any event, I'm getting too long in the tooth to play games!"

Winter turned to spring and without knowing it, or perhaps by preference, we had chosen to put out of our minds the un-resolved controversy of Molly's doll. That was until just several days ago whilst I was odd jobbing, namely storing unwanted win-ter essentials away in the spacious loft, surprising me and out of the blue I felt someone touch my arm. Glimpsing back over my shoulder into the dimness of the loft space I made out a small adolescent girl dressed head to toe in white cap and loose overall type smock. She began to talk in a high fast voice, pulling at her plaits as she spoke. I could tell they were the wrong words and not what she meant to say. Those wide-open eyes said it all.

In a little while I brought about consoling her and coaxing her to sit with me on the upturned wooden box. Her tiny voice had quelled to a whisper now as she eagerly shared an esoteric life and death with me.

Her name is Mercy Holgate and I am sure you will find her story intriguing. Mercy come and meet the family. Mercy straight away made a beeline for the self-same rocking chair that Peter Jackson had his sights on a few days ago – there is something comforting about rocking chairs isn't there? Speaking slow and trying not to stumble she began to spin it all out to us.

"Some people don't see what happens when they die, but I did. It all took place between twelve and one o'clock after my dad had been to the bank in his lunch hour and then on to pay Martin Le-Roy, the Funeral Director. I remember four men sliding the long narrow box on to the back of a two-wheeled trap and then leading the pony to the clearing where I was to be buried. It looked a very nice little spot. The men took the box to the edge of a hole and lowered it in with ropes. My little sister was too young to understand and I was pleased when mother lastly put her arms around her and held her close."

"I recall them singing a hymn that began 'Jesus, lover of my soul' then shortly after they all disappeared down a little curved path."

"My father owned the village dairy and I used to earn pocket money by delivering milk to the old parsonage – where you live now. When it started to fall into disrepair they located it nearer to the village. I was so happy when, after some time, your family made it their home – it was sad to see it in ruin."

"I was always fearful that I might get consumption again and that they would feed me with beef tea and white of egg to try and keep my strength up and so, after my parents moved on to Shapley, I moved into your parsonage with you."

"I was so happy and I loved to watch Molly playing with her dolls on the lawn in the summer and tucking them up to go to sleep."

"I enjoyed sharing your house, although oftentimes I felt that I didn't have the right; nevertheless I was too frightened to make myself known to you."

"The doll was meant to be a parting gift to Molly for all of the laughter and fine times. I think I am a mouse and a sissy on account of my helplessness to make myself leave and I am always left with an uncomfortable feeling of regret and a peculiar weariness that comes with my relaxation of effort. I am sorely sorry!"

When things are as persistent and inevitable as death and then somehow stumbling on the chance to live again it becomes difficult to say 'no' to a somewhat spunky girl … and so we didn't!

One day; but not today,
I'll make a pilgrimage
to Mercy Holgate's dusky mind
if only just to take her
this year's calendar.

Surely all of us need to know
what year it is we're living in?

32

Why am I me, and why not you?

'HI THERE' AND 'Dear John' have signified both the beginning and the ending of a romantic relationship in every part of everywhere throughout this century and the last one. Be that as it may, I was sad to learn that our gun toting highwayman Sid Martin and jazz singer supreme, the fractured Billie Holiday, had of late become downright scrappy. You would think that this clumsy and sorrowfully inept couple, separated by decades of cultural counterbalance, really wouldn't have a chance in courtship, but, on the contrary, until recently their ardour was blossoming. Not a logical conclusion, but then finality rarely is.

Perhaps I have taken an extraordinary stance by interfering in their 'lives'. Perhaps the quality of the heart should be the deciding factor. However, if only to put a positive spin on events, and to put a cheer on my readers' faces too, I opted to go straight to Abraham to seek his suggestions and conceivably a verdict.

Abraham is a wise old owl. In fact, even as a boy he was an 'old head on young shoulders'. Born in Dusseldorf, Germany in 1945 he narrowly missed the shindig that was WWII and thankfully the horror of the Holocaust too.

Although Abraham fortunately missed all of that evil and hostility by a hair's breadth, he told me that he still cannot help to sense the residue whenever he visits. He recalled for me that when he was a child of around 4 or 5 years he would often stop and watch some of the more unfortunate groups – children as well – sifting through the bomb damage for what by chance they might find. He says that oftentimes his mind was vacant aside from the re-occurring voice in his head "Why am I me and why not you – why am I here and why not there?"

Billie's dystopian vision of society, versus Sid's indistinguish-able vision of society, viz: Sex as a vehicle to more success versus the significance of guns and gore – perhaps this is the link, the loop, the connection? Somehow they both seemingly approach the worst aspects of themselves and of humanity with a simi-lar view; let's be honest, being 'really' happy together isn't always that great in any event. Periodically they should give that some thought. To cut a long story short, having a maimed left hand is a physical symbol of friend Sid's social handicap, whilst chewing gum at the same time as singing and discussing Sid's erection is Billies!

It just seems to me that there's some darn questions that have got easily available, almost ready-made answers, to them – and some that just haven't and that is why I came here today to seek counsel from my old friend Abraham.

Abraham told me that he would sensitively and diplomatically speak with them for me and at the same time left me with this thought:-

"In the event that Billie and Sid were 21st century adults with their exact same outlook, folks would most probably refer to them as being unconventional visionaries or somesuch. In some respects perhaps that is what they have become. Indeed, you have to be a wacko of sorts to have appreciated and to comprehend what's going down here at Hamptonia. Them being reborn is not an easy thing to grasp, either for you and me Ricky, or for Billie and Sid, is it?"

> I've been talking to the ceiling
> I've been talking to the floor
> and laughing at the shadow
> sneaking underneath the door.

33

Pola Negri (1897-1987)

"THE ACTION OF the scene was to make it look like I was chained to the railroad track and then just before the train came the stunt man would take over. The assistants had dug a hole under the track for him to slide into and the train would just go over the top."

I thought the stunt man looked a trifle absurd. He was a wiry and muscular man and wearing a white scarf and dress just like the ones I was wearing. In fact I thought it was absurd to let him do the scene when I could easily do it myself. "Wait a minute!" I yelled. "I can do this!"

The director tried hard to dissuade me, but my mind was made up, so they chained me up on the track leaving the chains loose so that I could slide easily into the hole. On the signal I heard the train whistle and the terrifying rumble of the engine as it began to move down the track. I slipped effortlessly out of the chain and slid into the hole. Moments later the sky over me was blacked out as the cowcatcher passed over me and then the screech of engine wheels stopping. When they lifted me out of the hole and I stood up in my little fluttering white dress all the team applauded. The director himself rushed straight over and kissed me – I felt wonderful.

Somehow the whole afternoon had just slipped nonchalantly by doing especially boring household tasks. I was looking forward to a hot shower and some clean clothes when I heard loquacious chatter coming from our sitting room.

I could see that Molly was all keyed up and quite excited. "Dad, this is my new best friend, Pola." Uninterrupted she continued "Pola this is my Dad."

"Pola has been telling me the most fabulous stories about her showbizzy life. Did you know she was once married to a genuine Marquis as well?"

Pola and me fittingly shook hands – it was almost as though she was prepared to be faced with meeting me – I on the other hand was not prepared!

"Sorry about my somewhat dishevelled appearance" I threw in my best and most appropriate apology. "Household chores, they never cease and I'm trying to quit smoking!"

Molly came to my aid as she started up again. "Like Mom, Pola is a very talented film actress and she sings too!"

"Oh Molly, I don't expect that I am anything near as talented as your Mom is." In an unusual depth of deprecation she added quickly "a director once told me I stink!"

From the evening of the same day we were all in turn routinely introduced to our new arrival Pola Negri. It kind of launched a reinvigorated supernatural involvement for us, inasmuch that Pola had the knack and tendency to give our ragbag household a buzz; whether individually or as a whole. Whereas I dare say we might have been described as an unpretentious bunch and to the limits of probability, we had endeavoured to stay that way too. Since becoming acquainted with Pola, we were beginning to discover that her kind of streak of unlifelike slapdash was rubbing off on us. Indeed, I don't think that there is anything wrong with a 'throw caution to the wind' type of attitude from time-to-time do you?

Just several evenings ago Katharine and me were laying in bed exchanging views and generally deliberating upon some of Pola's numerous 'adventures'! I told Katharine how I found it somewhat, if not extremely extraordinary, how Pola is deemed by us, and indeed accepted by us all, as being a more famous than most movie star, and yet just to set the record straight, I for one have never heard of her! I am not being judgemental here Katharine,

I am just curious that's all. There are many dead actresses that I adore and I've watched them in movies many times, but she isn't one of them Katharine!

Katharine propped herself up on her arm so that she could observe my quizzical expression and teasingly replied "that's because Pola Negri is slightly before your time dear Ricky – she was one of silent cinema's early trailblazers and a femme fatale no less! I should watch yourself Ricky" she added with a cheeky smile on her face.

Katharine always was too quick witted by far!

I like movies because
I never see myself in them
I see the dreams of people
who look like spooks and cowboys
and who act like children.

– Ricky Dale –

34

"There are more things in heaven and earth Horatio than are dreamt of in your philosophy"

IT WAS FOR sure the hottest darn British summer that I have ever known.

Abraham and me sat in the shade of a cluster of massive oak trees that adorned what was once an ornamental garden to our house. He was repeatedly fanning himself with his white straw hat, like it might do some good, and we both sipped upon my summertime concoction of gin and iced grapefruit juice – and it really did do some good!

"Like someone once said" he snarkly remarked "ninety-nine degrees in the shade and there ain't much shade! You got to stop feeding me such indulgent servings of your gin Ricky, it tends to go to my head and makes me too damned testy – it's too hot to be testy, it's just too hot period."

"Not too hot to get a wee bit inebriated" I said, standing up to fetch more ice, "which I have every intention of doing whilst the girls are stopping over in the city for the night."

"Seriously dear Abraham, I need to use this set of circumstances to run something past you. Fundamentally, it's stuff that has been tumbling around my head ever since Katharine returned home several months ago. To be quite honest with you, for the past month or more I've averaged about four hours sleep a night – oh my health is excellent and my mental state couldn't be better; the uncontrollable root of my worry is Katharine."

Abraham had summoned his committed face, the one not frequently seen except when a friend urgently asks for help!

"I have heard of many a queer thing" said Abraham "I have known men to fall in love with girls so ugly that you wonder if their eyes are straight, so do tell Ricky, do tell!"

"I am terrified Abraham. I am totally transfixed on the thought of losing Katharine. I cannot go through that process again! You see, it's difficult for me to just accept that my Katharine is in the here and now, when her being here wholly and entirely defies all logic and reason."

"The first thing is Ricky, try not to deny God. My question to you is why have you found it necessary to suddenly turn your back on him?"

"So, what are you suggesting my dear friend, that if I trust in him everything will always turn out alright? Ok then Abraham…, I'll say five Hail Marys, three Acts of Contrition and two Our Fathers four times daily for a month, and then will God step in and take over my life and then will God find an eternity for both my Katharine and me?"

"Same old questions and answers dear Ricky. Just for once I'd like to hear some brand-new questions and answers that don't necessarily result in you having to start shouting hallelujahs to an unseen choir or indeed whispering spondulicks of fado's under your breath for either you to believe in God or vice versa."

Abraham hadn't finished, not by a long chalk as he took his somewhat fuzzy logic the distance – I was pleased to know that at least he wasn't at a loss for words!

"Ricky my friend" he said as he looked straight into my eyes "we know that there is plenty to bitch about in this intolerant and intolerable world that we call home. For sure Jesus was well aware of this fault in mankind. However, his dad, our Lord, is either in depressive denial of the facts or his son's balls haven't dropped yet enough to alert his dad of the problems and that it's not 'job done' yet – in fact far from it!"

"It seems to me he/they should exert themselves and try asking the 'five bucks a dance' girls, or the ditzy youngsters with successive adoptive parents, all about the sorrow and contradictions in their world, and then afterwards Ricky take yourself to a quiet place and seriously ask yourself the question 'how can I possibly deny the existence of God?' I ask you who else but God could 'fuck up' in such an impressive and totally magnificent style dear Ricky?"

"Ok Abraham, putting God to one side for a moment, the last time we spoke you mentioned that your theory for explaining the materialization of our so-called ghosts or visitors relied entirely upon the essence of time. Inasmuch that time past, present and future all co-exist in an infinity of multiple parallel universes – one on top of the other, or perhaps better put, one concurrent with another. If my mind serves me right, you proposed that when an alive person (us) 'sees' a ghost or visitor, we are looking out from our time frame and observing events in another time frame. My question to you dear scholarly friend is how is it feasible or at least within reason that our ghosts/visitors are able to experience exactly the self-same emotions – love, pain, shock – as we do if they are little more than a vision or figment?"

"I will give it my best shot to answer that question for you Ricky. These 'ghosts' (not unlike our dear Katharine) primarily visit us through a break in the continuum of time. In other words Ricky, although on occasions though fleeting their visits may be, they are definitely still alive when we interact together – at least they are in their time system. Hypothetically, if we see, touch, speak to a manifestation of a person dressed as though they are in the 1890s, it is simply the case that they are still in the 1890s, but have stepped, maybe unknowingly, into our time zone. In short, they are alive as you and me when we interact with them, however exclusively in their time zone only."

"This is a really interesting theory of yours Abraham, one that

I think I could wrestle with, however, I am not going to
put my weight behind it until you answer this. How come we
never receive any 'visitors' from the future?"

Abraham looked at me with a kind of childish smirk on his
face. "I did hear tell a report about a young fella who was being
frequented by an apparition of his elderly self – wildly fascinating
stuff eh?"

"Have you ever read any of Lewis Carroll's stories Ricky? I'll
bet you've got at least one book there on your shelves. Molly
would know. Ask her about the part in Alice Through the Looking Glass where Alice enters the flipped world on the other side
of her mirror and discovers that memory does not only go backwards, it also has the ability to remember what's going to happen
the week after next! I guess that's what 'magic' mushrooms and
such will do for you!"

Abraham was beginning to irritate my train of thought by his
superfluous digressing. Intent on getting back on track I chose
to mention an article I had read by The Society for Psychical
Research who reported many instances of dead people who appeared to be trying to establish communication with the living…

"So my question is dear Abraham, how can the dead be privy
to such knowledge about the living?"

Abraham gave me a small-bore sideways look and muttered
"perhaps they have stool pigeons in God's heaven Ricky!"

I guess at that point I decided we'd been gestating for long
enough – sustained by gin and cigarettes; conceivably enough was
enough for now. Me, being a last word freak, I just threw in one
last sentence for my friend.

"The certainty is Abraham, that some kind of non-physical
communication is taking place between us and them."

He chimed in "Pass me another drink dear Ricky and I'll try to
answer your conundrum in one for you and Katharine."

"This sense of 'being' that the dead folks have seems to me

to be totally independent of the body or of any normal operation/function of the brain. That being the case it gives rise to the concept of the soul, or call it what you will – soul, spirit, personality – this separate entity survives death as we know it and can still communicate in the self-same transcendental way as it would have during life."

Abraham was undeniably spot on with his 'unearthly' summing up of the topic. I showed my complete agreement by a series of stony-faced nods; nevertheless, dogged as I am to having the last word, I just simply added "Amen!"

> *We are indeed pawns, condemned to move only forward*
> *through time and as a result we have little knowledge and*
> *understanding of the wider world.*
>
> – Abraham Stern –

35
A day in the life of Ricky Dale

I WENT TO my doctor this morning for one of those terrible once a year check-ups that they like the over 60s to have. It's the kind of check up where they do virtually nothing and they waste their valuable time just the same. My doc went out of his room briefly to attend an elderly lady who had fainted and regrettably she spilled her glass of water on him. When he came back it looked as though he'd peed himself!

On the way home a moron stopped me in the street and asked "you're that author aren't you?" He accented 'author' as 'aufer' which, just for an instant, endeared him to me. Then he asked "maybe you can help me?" From then on the conversation worsened. I said what was it because I was in a sort of a hurry and he said he had written some children's stories and could I publish them for him and then he asked "by the way what's your name?"

My younger brother Mike (Vince to his friends!) telephoned me at around 2.30pm, him having just gotten out of bed, to let me know about a new movie project he was very athletically involved in as a participant! The film, starring his new Danish model girlfriend, centred around about fifty nude girls serving hotdogs and beer and culminated in some frenzied mud splashing and wrestling.

Our Mike's done well and made himself a whole lot of dough. You just wouldn't believe that he started out dressed as Robin Hood (including bow and arrows) liberally giving away glasses of cider in a superstore. Don't think he's in line for an Oscar just yet though!

In the evening Abraham and Esther, Molly, Katharine and me had accepted an invitation from our local pub landlord to judge the Madonna 'singing and look alike' contest. The landlord had somewhat optimistically expected at least a dozen girls to attend. However only four turned up so it was all over pretty fast. Shame though, because the girls had obviously spent a fortune on clothes and jewellery. I took the Boots voucher prize over to the winner. She was sat with some eunuch of gorilla proportions looking thoroughly pissed off and drawing cocks on her beer mat – kind of Madonnaesque I thought!

On the late news that evening the headline was how the police had busted a paedophile ring in West Yorkshire. It showed them being put into the Black Maria with bags on their heads to hide their faces. I cannot fully understand why these immensely wicked individuals have a so-called 'special right' to anonymity and indeed are legally protected from their faces being made public. Only the dead are entitled to that eccentric blessing!

Remaking the world

Towards the end
when one was all
and all was one
and God
was forever stammering
A non-extremist guy
came to him and said
'Oh God, just give me
a weekly magazine,
a radio
and a TV set
and I'll create the world for you
just the way you want it.

God,
although rather surprised
that so little was required
for such a large undertaking
immediately agreed to give
him what was needed.

The next day, while Eve
watched television
Cain wrote the editorial
for the magazine
and Abel tried to find
the right channel for
pop music,
Adam, fully aware
of his actions
set out
towards Heaven.

36

Codename: Operation Menu

MOLLY RECOGNISED THE man's face instantly despite the fact that he was noticeably a great deal more youthful looking than of late.

He looked at her with a pleased and friendly expression certain that analytically she was trying to bring valid reasoning to this weird set of circumstances.

His 'spur of the moment impetuousness' was that of a young man as he began to get what had happened off his chest. He was unrelenting in his offensive language regarding President Nixon; there was a moment when Molly thought he may have talked himself hoarse!

Molly watched mesmerized as he paused and reached into his combat vest for a pack of Camel and she caught sight of the man's name – Abraham Stern – engraved upon the lapel of his pocket. The shock by the confirmation that she was right made her feel kind of light and vacant for a moment – and it was only for a moment because she asked "I wonder how long it would have taken for me to have found out who you were?" They just looked at each other questioningly.

"You are Katharine and Ricky's daughter" he said respectfully. "What did they name you?"

"Molly" she answered and felt pleased that he had asked.

"Molly, it seems certain that our partial parallel universes have seriously become messed up. There are some common points that are still connected, but the greater number are divided by a makeshift stop gap. I guess I am wandering between two worlds, one dead and the other not far off dead – and then there's me trying to tell one from the other! Perhaps hidden amongst mind and matter is a kind of filigree that once woven, and with time, will become my final world."

He smiled a nice smile, an authentic close smile and added "At least I found my way home to you all." Molly was perking up now and just shook her head in a way that might have meant either yes or no.

They sat at the kitchen table and drank hot coffee out of blue willow cups. The room was cool and the half-drawn shades softened the glare of the daybreak from the windows. He took out of his rucksack a large tin box that contained a small loaf of bread, some oranges and cheese. He did not eat that much, but sat leaning back in his chair as if for an untroubled instant he had almost found his tranquility.

His 'spur of the moment impetuousness' was as follows:-

President Nixon authorised a covert USAF Strategic Air Command bombing campaign conducted in eastern Cambodia from March '69 to May '70.

Previously intended as Operation Breakfast, it came to be known as Operation Menu.

During one intense bombing air strike Abraham Stern's bomber and crew were lost.

The American command were confident it was winning and the war would soon be over. In the latter sense they were right. The war was very much over for the increasing number of dead like Abraham Stern who were repatriated back to the States!

Where is the place at which I choose to embark? Is it somewhere between a past half forgotten and a future as yet only glimpsed – can there be one without the other?

Molly, on behalf of Abraham

37
In another time, some things don't change

AUTUMN REALLY SUITS England and it most especially suits Devonshire where the countryside and the sea faithfully engage with one another and you never have to laboriously seek one out without finding the other.

At around 6a.m. in this part of the country, when the wind is high and the sky for the most part starless, moonless and disastrously black, there is no finer place in the world to be. By the time I've stepped outside, closed and locked the front door and looked up again at the sky, little stabs of brightness are beginning to be interspersed through the misty clouds and trying ever so hard to break through.

Yeah, decidedly I was out and about early this morning. Early and kind of lazily struggling with the prospect of taking my customary 'constitutional'. Perhaps the coast path this morning? Meandering along the cliff edge kind of appealed to me and exhilarated my sense of adventure somewhat; the smell of the ocean, the dipping and weaving of the gulls – to a simple hometown boy, all of these things matter immensely to me.

There are a number of country benches scattered intermittently along my cliff walk. Most are mossy and antiquated and in a sad state of repair. However, for trekkers and footsloggers alike they are a lifeline to pause and recover. This particular a.m. I was seriously stepping it out, lively and quite devoid of workaday stuff and benches!

Apart from focussing on negotiating the slippery path, Bebop's disappearance was bothering me somewhat. As a rule as soon as he saw me he would have been racing to the front door.

I kind of speculated on whether Molly had allowed him to sleep in her room?

To my complete surprise, as I rounded the corner avoiding some stinging nettle bushes, I unexpectedly came upon Father Humphrey. He was sitting silently on a shambly bench and right by his side sat a young girl who I assumed may be Lynne. In almost malleable muteness the pair of them were gazing out to sea.

"Come and check out the soft red sunrise with us Ricky!" There was a kind of joyfulness in his voice and, without bothering to look around at me, he continued "see yours and our shadows Ricky? They are moving in tune to time. If you pay close attention you may observe years pass within a single hour." Then he began to witter on to me further, like this unconventional 'pow wow' we were having had some purpose or objective to it.

"Did you know Ricky that the Romantic painters deliberately avoided the classical habit at that time of dividing the land and the sea with a clear line of horizon? Instead they preferred to combine both land and sea in a state or situation of horrid confused movement and turmoil. Often the spectator would be placed at the heart of a perilous water's edge. Turner even painted the awe-inspiring Land's End with glowering skies and jagged bare rocks below." Then quickly he added "Check out the soft red sunrise just once more will you Ricky – an absolute identical of the first sunrise, except on this occasion your and my shadows are stillborn" – he turned around and looked at me for the first time "It's on account that this second sunrise belongs to a particular period of time that does not belong to us. You see Lynne here Ricky, she is not dead, she is very much alive, watch her shadow, it's moving!"

"Lynne hasn't and may never have her serendipitous mishap in my Bell Tower, and your Katharine has never owned a horse whose name was Hamptonia. It is all about avoiding certain time frames and if you are lucky they will both enjoy the long

109

lives they deserve!"

"Most dead folks are unmistakably, positively dead Ricky. I have no evidence indicating whether my theory is true or valid, but it seems to me that the so-called dead individuals that you, me and perhaps others are encountering are not in fact deceased, they are ostensibly folk who are very much alive, but somehow exist in a different offbeat time frame to us."

"Can you imagine the irony Ricky that some of the folk who visit you may have come to the same conclusion as we have? Others my friend will have most probably assumed that you are a ghost, in the same way as you once believed and perceived them to be!"

An ode to Father Humphrey

Whatever moral tract
or bulging Bible
gave him rules and regulations
to abide by;
preordained or predestined
he learned that practice well.

Needless to say I was in very deep thought as I made my way home that autumn morning. I stumbled on the truth and at the same time I became aware of an emotional side of me I didn't know existed. Descriptively it was like returning to my home and family after being lost in a hinterland of nowhere for years – I felt almost as if I was a stranger. I guess that in most respects I wasn't really taking 'the crisis' that well. I was just plain and simply scared! I guess what I truly needed was a crazy old fortune-teller complete with crystal ball and handprinted business cards 'Madam Zena – the Past – the Present – the Future'. It was all just too much too soon for this hometown boy to cope with!

I glanced briefly at the name on the gatehouse which read 'The Parsonage'. Quite an innocuous name, except it should have read 'Hamptonia'! It seems to me that from now onwards I needed to take heed of these little subtleties as they were likely to be a precise indicator of what sub-division of time I was about to find myself in.

Fortunately my key still fitted the lock. Success I thought, my front door had endured the fullness of time!

Once inside our home looked astonishingly, yet somewhat unsettlingly, much the same as I had left it earlier that morning. It would have been difficult not to have noticed that the 2x3 portrait of Katharine which I had hung above the mantelpiece had ceased to exist – after Katharine's death I had purposely requisitioned an artist to paint her portrait using publicity photos lent to me by her studio.

What was striking though was that, although the order of our chattels were primarily unchanged, nevertheless the whole darn caboodle of stuff appeared to be so clean, fresh and new. Indeed, unspoilt by probably two decades of use. It's strange the little inconsequential piffling things that draw your attention, like the stair carpet which hadn't worn thin yet!

Entering our bedroom I was trying to make little or no noise. However, Katharine was wide awake tapping her palm upon the thick soft quilt and motioning me toward our bed. She spoke only as I got close, softly in almost a whisper. It was almost as if she was about to reveal some huge confidential secret to me, but perhaps that was just my exaggerated paranoia over what had occurred!

"I've given Molly her feed, burped her and put her down – go see how absolutely divine our baby looks Ricky, go take a peek" and then almost sorrowfully shamefaced she added "We are so, so fortunate to be parents of such a dear sweet child." It was Katharine's 'as if by default' remark that caused me to quake a bit, viz "watch over her Ricky." I murmured something in reply, but I can't remember what it was I said.

I tippy-toed over to see Molly. She looked so small and help-less curled up at the bottom of her high slatted crib. It sure was not easy to take on board that just several hours ago she had caringly yelled "Goodnight Dad!" from her bedroom at the top of the stairs.

For all one knows our lives present and our lives past are not at all that dissimilar in nature, inasmuch that the constant denom-inator is 'love' and only desperation cuts through both time, space and everything.

38

Blind Obsession

To all intents and purposes Katharine had virtually given up her professional activities since the birth of our daughter Molly some ten years ago. However, from time to time, she was not aloof to accepting an invitation to come out of her self-imposed retirement if it suited her financial disposition, or moreover if it was beneficial to Molly. With Christmas approaching fast, combined with Katharine's 'infliction' toward buying Molly nice things, Katharine was indeed open to sensible offers.

Just several weeks before Christmas 1980 the telephone rang. It was her former agency saying that there was a rock star in town who particularly wanted to have her on his imminent album cover – with him! He turned out to be Ric Ocasek from the Cars.

She outlined the days events for me over a rum and coke after she'd returned home that evening:-

"He was not that good-looking Ricky; he had lots of gold earrings and beautifully white capped teeth and dyed black long hair." She added "He was terribly sweet and charming though – like David Bowie is!"

It was late so I had a taxi cab pick me up and take me to the railway station to meet Katharine upon her return. She was un-surprisingly very tired and to some extent still slightly fazed by the John Lennon shooting which had happened just a few days earlier. She mentioned how saddened she was for Yoko and at that point our cab driver went full-on about it all.

"Don't worry John baby, we're all up there with you" he solemnly remarked.

Katharine's comeback put me in mind of a response at Mass

"Not me John" she said "I'm stayin' right f'in down here!" Under the circumstances all that I could add was "ditto!"

Be that as it may, my dear Katharine had thoroughly enjoyed her lengthy jaunt to London and back. "Catching up on all of the blether blather and scandalous goings on" she remarked with a diminutive smile on her face. For my part in the plot, I didn't really give a damn if Mia was going to marry Woody, etc. I heard that Ric Ocasek was overjoyed with the final proofs of the photo shoot and moreover he was tickled pink by Katharine's 'English-ness' – and why wouldn't he be?

When I picked Katharine up from the railway station and heard her say "hello", it was as though we had just met. She was the entirety of everything I wanted to possess; I knew no one worth my envying.

On the morning she left I spent several hours trying to neaten the garden and once I'd managed to straighten up from that, I began to make a secret list of pretty things for Katharine's and Molly's Christmas.

It was late afternoon and I made the unsound decision to visit the grave yard. Especially one tombstone, so stiff and so straight, standing there like a stark, definitive sentinel of time.

Worry and fear; the two familiars that still walk beside me. In the face of it all I am certain that there may be no escape for us, despite Father Humphrey's extraordinary revelations!

39

Evaluation

IT SEEMS TO me that Father Humphrey's inappropriately named 'revelations' may not in fact be a huge mismatch between the logical and illogical – in spite of my leanings in any other way. It also seems to me that my 'all important' role in metaphorically or otherwise deciding life and death – refusing to admit or accept – is my lily-livered opt out of avoiding a decision. I haven't either the belief or conviction to denounce the good Father's hypothesis or indeed decry what he has told me on the basis of my trepidation and fearfulness. Notwithstanding what I saw, I saw vividly with my own eyes – a revelation if ever there was one!

All-in-all I ask where does this leave me? Exhausted and all over the place, that's where. What's more, I hasten to add), on the basis of any type of evidence to the contrary, it is most likely that Father Humphrey's 'assumptions' are most ridiculously accurate.

So why then am I in denial? Perhaps because I am living each day out in a supposedly double negative framework. Not only but also, I exist in a periodic, recurring portion of time that is spanning over two decades. This, combined with associations of interchangeable identity, does not lend itself to be the idyllic life that I imagined!

The question that I often ask myself of late and needs to be resolved asap, is how and what sets the whole kit and caboodle of all this mystical bugaboo into motion and why? Explicitly crystal clear is that an unknown highly developed system or cunning technique triggers it all. Perhaps some unpleasant bent circumstance in time or a delusional genius – most likely believably yet so preternaturally far-fetched! On the other hand the concept of a totally natural phenomena – such as clouds or wind – that are given to having a spontaneously energized temperament may not be that far off the mark.

For a smalltown boy with the indigent disadvantage of not having a degree in psychokinesis, quantum mechanics and such as a choice – ad litem I am tearfully and exasperatedly stuffed!

40

A mare's nest!

So, PERHAPS WE have the benefit of both worlds, differing situations, enjoyed at the same time. We have all that belongs to a particular period, but not necessarily the abundance of all the people we knew. For example, what should be taking place in 'bang up to date' time is Esther and Abraham's visit – that is to say vacationing at the spooky house with Molly and myself. Can you believe that of late we are attempting to make sense of and find an explanation to all of the 'spooky' jiggery pokery that occurs here on a regular basis? 'Reason' and 'purpose' being our bywords.

Although theoretically to everyone, except me, the supposition of another life is as Abraham might say 'kosher'.

Count back the months slowly and it is likely you can reach a destination in Esther and Abraham's alternate lives that even they are oblivious to viz: Lieutenant Abraham Stern and his crew have been lost in a Cambodian air strike. Esther Stern has moved away from their USAF base apartment and has put back to her home in Louisiana; memo dated June 10 1969.

And what of my Katharine? At any moment in time Katharine is flittering and fussing here, there and eventually almost everywhere in all sorts of forms, guises and beguiling disguises. Alert, active and alive, that's Katharine; ditto, ditto and departed, that's Katharine too. Katharine the actress who claims her inspiration comes whilst soaking in the bath tub – Katharine the mother who claims her best ideas come whilst washing dishes and drying them. Apparently the renowned Raymond Chandler was quoted as saying that he found stimulation by watching his wife clean house in the nude – I can identify with that! However, I'll bet she didn't dash back and forth through the unexplained ravages of life and death like my Katharine does!

Immediately preceding is our Molly, who oftentimes exits as a grown-up and double-quick manifests anew as our adored little-bitty baby. Things are becoming so convoluted of late that it's unclear whether to warm her baby feed or pour her a pina colada!

None of the aforementioned kinships are strained in any respect. On the contrary I idolize these souls, living or dead, but there have come many occasions recently when I ask myself the question "do I have what it takes to effectively cope with what's going on?" I have actually begun to seriously question my integrity and particularly my personal interpretation and perhaps exploitation of the term 'truth' inasmuch, will I ever have the inner strength to reveal the 'truth' to my loved ones and, in the event that I do decide to reveal it, how will our relationships be affected as a result?

41

Bricks and Mortar

'DEAR MR DALLY' the letter began; a two-paragraph single spaced letter written with typical inaccuracy upon an old Bar-let typewriter – that was my guess, and definitely not a computer; not in those days in any event.

Isn't it odd how bureaucratic mail always has a foreboding about it and yet going against my uneasiness, this particular letter was in fact the good news on which we had pinned all our hopes upon.

It was just before Molly was born and Katharine and me had put all of our savings into purchasing this anachronistic, well-nigh derelict parsonage. We thought of it as an investment and intended to renovate it into several first home apartments. I guess the venture was always reliant upon the city fathers giving the green light – and right now, sitting on red plastic chairs, leaning over a plastic table holding plastic cups with insipid 'stores special' coffee, our future was very much in the balance!

Silence ruled as I opened and began to read the contents of the letter to Katharine. Just before I'd gotten to the 'yours sincerely' one more strange phenomenon began to steal in and take control, not quickly, not slowly, more like inwardly.

Our investment had divided and multiplied into several reasonably pleasant apartments. Like a living organism the inorganic had become organic. Given the issue's complexity, a summary for my reader is difficult, primarily because in the light of it all, I can only assume the facts and not ever establish the facts. One thing is certain though, these so-called 'procreative' situations do in fact put one in a more favourable position. I need to be sure it's in everyone's interests though – fait accompli is not an option!

42

The end game

A QUOTE FROM Chapter 37...

> *"There are a number of country benches scattered*
> *intermittently along my cliff walk, most are mossy and*
> *antiquated and in a sad state of repair. However, for*
> *trekkers and foot sloggers alike they are a lifeline to pause*
> *and recover"...*

It was around 6a.m. and I had a hunch that I would most probably find Father Humphrey and Lynne gazing out to sea.

"Have you come to check out this morning's sunrise with us Ricky?" he remarked in his best 'come to church' voice. Still not bothering to look around at me he continued "What a discreditable race of beings we all have become Ricky. We truly want to make sense of what we see all around us and yet we are lazy and more content to go about our putrid daily lives understanding only what we deem necessary to understand – which is basically nothing. Where did it all come from Ricky, why nature is the way it is, where indeed did the cosmos originate? Do we lack intelligence Ricky or are we unable to think clearly through lack of effort?"

Inadvertently I am sure, but he was beginning to hold my own views and so I deliberately plunged right into the conversation.

"Father, you and I and Lynne are blatantly aware that time per se flows backwards in a more explicit order than it flows forward. Furthermore that by reason of this, effects can often precede causes. My question to you both is that why then do I clearly remember the past when I am in the past and yet I have no comprehension of the future?"

Lynne looked at me and smiled. She understood precisely where I was coming from, however it was Father Humphrey who dived in with his reply. "Your question is even more difficult to answer than you imagine Ricky, particularly for me because I also have my religious precepts to grapple with. So, instead I will refer you to a similar question that Einstein asked with regard to whether God had any choice in creating the universe? My own opinion is Ricky that I think he did!" Father Humphrey grinned from ear to ear and added "Withal any creator has to have something to do doesn't he Ricky – even you are aware of that?"

"In any event I am relocating, even before the lark has ascended!" he said raising his voice "and I am taking Lynne along with me. She needs a fresh start. The Bishop has given me a diocese that is less discombobulated. I seized the opportunity Ricky, even the church has no explanation for the unbalance in this vicinity."

"Ricky, the church has many eloquent discourses to use as persuasion, none of which I intend to use. Please though heed my words, as your friend, and take your little family far away from this ill-fated acreage – scoot Ricky whilst you have the will and opportunity to do so. I earnestly implore you to heed my words. This place will eventually become your nemesis Ricky and the more you confront it the more its portals of evil will devour you. I know that the 'all important' factor to making your decision will be whether you can change things as they actually are to being how you might like them to be. No one really knows the ocean Ricky unless they're sinking into it. The shore is only shore if you don't walk from it. It is apparent there is nothing we can do to change the status quo that has existed for perhaps thousands of years, you should take your family and go Ricky."

I looked at Father Humphrey with a new kind of makeshift mysticism and, although I realised his intentions were genuine,

I really wanted to broach the subject further with him before I decided what to do. That afternoon we had tea together and this is how he outlined it for me and for my reader too:-

"The future and past are so ingeniously constructed inasmuch that lettered folk, dispassionate scholars and even the more puritanical among us cannot grasp the astute mosaic of its mechanism. On account of being faced with so many unexplainable inconsistencies, as is often the case, they withdraw into the snail-shell of their more traditional and familiar world. However, that's exactly what we didn't do isn't it Ricky? We wanted at least a few answers! Problem being that some of these answers are dead-weight (no pun intended) and not necessarily the way we would prefer to envisage them."

"Are you conversant with the term 'energy highway' Ricky? Perhaps more commonly referred to as 'Ley Line'. It spans across some 364 miles from east to west covering the whole length of Cornwall, through Devon and even into some parts of Wiltshire. From check outs I've made this so-called Ley Line is most likely the key to actually unlocking the matrix of how, where and why space, time, future and past and indeed life and death are all linked and meticulously shaped. Be that as it may, at some important point in antiquity the Line has become damaged, maybe even severed, the point of the fracture being our acreage. The damage to the Line inadvertently created the most powerful vortex through which the dead can travel and it all culminates at your property and mine Ricky. Apparently in bygone times our acreage was given the title of 'Corpse Valley'!"

"I guess the only good news is that due to the fracture, the dead are unable to return along the Ley Line, however they are able to form and develop into life-like composites of themselves and that's when they visit us Ricky!"

"The strength of evidence is somewhat mind boggling, but nevertheless awfully compelling. My predecessor Father Runyon apparently used the energy portal to connect with two ancient churches nearby. Where this portal is now is anyone's guess, but I remember him telling me it had 'healing' properties. It most probably did inasmuch that when he died, he used the portal and Ley Line to his advantage."

"We have been occupying a space in seemingly our own private little country Ricky; a country not drawn on any map. I know you don't want to run from it Ricky and desert that privilege with which you have grown used to all these many years. Me too! I've forged many alliances since I took over from Father Runyon, some with the most vulnerable and fragile parts of society. We have both taken a certain pride of living on the furthermost boundaries of death."

"Father Runyon came to me for confession just before he departed this world. He explained to me that inside of him was a judge who so far had remained silent and this judge had no intention of sentencing him until his last breath. Ask yourself this question Ricky. Do you want to wait until your last breath before you know whether or not you are doomed to wander through this valley for all eternity or, my friend, would you prefer to leave now of your own free will?"

I never have imagined that one day I would leave this place of my own volition or indeed that my wife, daughter and compadres wouldn't struggle in the slightest against my decision to leave here. Perhaps in some respects, like Father Humphrey, I was just the bearer of a message between two worlds – to all intents and purposes, very different worlds.

I willed this pleasant journey, at the time I thought it too wonderful to miss. I became the go-between, a kind of semi-celestial nonconformist with no professed beliefs other than that of the world with itself.

The end

An ode to us…

If we were to begin again
If today was yesterday
Could we forgive our doubts
Would we then act differently?

And just supposing yesterday were today
And right this moment
Is the beginning of a new week
How then would we act in our forgiveness?

If indeed forgiveness is what the future requires from us
(and that future is hastening close)
They why hasn't the past explained itself
At least more clearly?

Or perhaps this past is merely the commencement
Of a permanent present
And the permanent present
A cancellation of the future?

Sometimes it seems to me that the future
Has already passed
And instinctively it has become
An overtone to the present.

So surely if we are able to offer forgiveness
For both past and present
Then conceivably we might achieve
That forgiveness in the future?
Perhaps unwittingly
Our future relies upon
Forgiveness of the present
And a new beginning to the past?

I knew the bride when she used to rock n roll

ADDENDUM

KATHARINE, MOLLY AND me, together with our fine friends Esther and Abraham had spent the majority of the subsequent days quickly loading our belongings into the back of a hire vehicle. We decided to leave behind all of the heavy and bulky items and took only the necessities and essentials like some of our beloved chattels and of course our books. Even so, we soon filled up the whole truck to overflowing.

Bebop enjoyed all the commotion and kerfuffle and seemed to spend the whole day excitedly racing and bounding up and down the driveway in awareness and approval of what we were up to.

Esther and Abraham set their sights on spending several days and nights at the local Holiday Inn before eventually returning to their home. "It's located right by the Drakes statue and Plymouth Hoe" she enthused, as only a Louisianna lady could.

Katharine, Molly and me had arranged with my brother Mike to temporarily live at his hotel in Bournemouth – it wasn't really much of an hotel per se, more like useful accommodation if you are stuck! However, it was clean and homely and Molly simply idolized her Uncle Mike. I guess that being out of the clutches of that spooky house made us feel that the world really was our oyster again.

It was just turning dimsicle time when we finally pulled out of the driveway for the last time. Thankfully it was Molly who remembered that we'd forgotten to turn off both the water and electricity at the mains. Straight away I stopped the van and jogged back down the winding driveway to the old house. Expecting to see it in darkness the way we had left it a few minutes ago, I was somewhat taken aback to find that the whole building had become an amazing hive of activity. Actually it had become 'party time' at the old house. Music, dancing and generally a lot of so-called dead folk seemingly having fun!

I don't really understand why, but almost instinctively I felt as if I was barging in and interrupting an event that wasn't any longer my concern or my responsibility.

I immediately turned to leave and headed down the long meandering driveway from which I had just come when, kind of out of the blue, came this exact facsimile of Ricky Dale. He passed so close by that I could have easily reached out and touched him on the head and said 'Hi Ricky!'

I raised it with Katharine and our Molly later that evening because I recalled thinking at the time that perhaps Ricky number 2 was in fact my doppelganger. But there again, if by chance he was my doppelganger, surely he would have noticed me and said something?

Having said all of that, why in truth should he be obliged to acknowledge me, withal I am a person he does not know from Adam and outsiders are not normally encouraged or invited to come to this type of incongruous soiree in any event!

Have you read any of Ricky Dale's other work?

Here are some random snippets as itsy-bitsy appetizers and various readers' comments to reflect upon.

Please read on …

Poems (out of print) 1977
Limberlost 2011
Limberlost II The Legacy 2015
Limberlost III The Prequel 2016
Cloudburst 2019
The House on Dundas & Vine (work in progress) 2021

POEMS – 1977

Irish Lament
Vietnam Epitaph
The Barrack Room
Ode to Government
Island Heritage
War Mirages

and various other poems; fundamentally touching on the principles of democracy. Original paperback is out of print – only typed manuscripts are available.

Appreciation for Poems – 1977

"Ricky Dale enjoys an easy and fluid writing style and a sure ear for the rhythms of contemporary speech; dialogue, in particular internal, is well crafted; this supports the book substantially and advances the narrative"

(C J Bellamy, Newton Abbot, Devon, England)

LIMBERLOST – 2011

SHE STOOD IN the wings, among the tinfoil and stars, waiting for the introduction. "Don't let me do it alone Sandra, be right here" she whispered in a faint voice. Her face was ashen as the moment suddenly came to life and she walked out into centre stage; the curtain was hung in the middle to make the stage look smaller, but even so she looked frail and lost.

The light dimmed and the spotlight burst upon her in unity; she stood motionless, hiding behind her bold dark spectacles and watching the blue haze of tobacco smoke as it rose, twirled and fell. As though she has just emerged from some primeval darkness, there was a deafening silence; the entire auditorium seemed to have become tongue-tied in a deadlock of disbelief.

With the virtuality of some divine intervention the whole theatre suddenly lit up in a roaring frenzy like a cathedral on fire, but these were not sacrificial flames; she was once again Canada's Babylonian Queen, their courtesan, and they were on their feet to salute her like a pack of respectful howling wolves under a sky of love. Tears flowed, the walls shook and the floor reverberated in welcome and then, swift and utter silence.

There was an abnormal intrinsic quality to her performance. She had extended the range of her voice, breathing and conveying emotion to a pitch close to mania itself. Never like this had any audience understood and identified with another person's pain. Her lungs battered the air with such monumental sincerity. She sang in a total delirium of communication with every possible and powerful instinct available to her. It was the most stimulating and emotionally draining reciprocal union of compassion and spirit. Her voice was the embodiment of speech and music and perpetual suffering; a self-transformation of language; the singer's restless search for herself and the uniqueness of her being.

The performance concluded and Sandra frantically ran across stage to hold her. Her arms collapsed around Sandra like a weeping angel.

Appreciation for Limberlost – 2011

"A poignant story – a moving 'narrative of events' filled with simplicity, intertwined with complex emotion, eloquently and intelligently written"

(Diane Letky former magazine publisher – Montreal, Canada)

"Compelling, beautifully sentimental and sensitively written – almost spiritual"

(Rosemary Merrell, Devon, England)

LIMBERLOST II THE LEGACY – 2015

As if to interpret the significance of warmer weather, the furry snowflakes fell large and lazy throughout the day. It was the first of three long snow days and no colder than a winter Florida morning.

Each journey to the wood shed was surprisingly tedious and inhibited as the snow balled on their feet and the wet flakes festooned their clothing and soaked them in its melt.

The river was high and rising and the swift current clamoured thick and full with floating snow and slush ice.

The end of winter had all the earmarks of another delicate spring in the making; it was as though spring's determination to supersede was causing winter's last stand fretful pangs of remorse and generally throwing it into disarray.

The furry snowflakes unabatingly descended like eccentric dancing ghosts; this had become winter's swansong, beleaguered and bullied by the unfaltering murmuring of spring's ruffling impatience.

Another morning of another day and, like the landscape, there are never really endings only new beginnings and sometimes unanswered questions and tolerance for unclear reasons, and curiosity for the reasons of improbabilities and the inevitabilities and the nature of chance.

Appreciation for Limberlost II The Legacy – 2015

"I was in 'hogheaven' all the way through – in a caring, wistful way of course!"

(M Peters, Dorset, England)

"I have been struck by the sheer intensity of what I think could best be described as the author's 'poetic' style. By this I mean that much of the prose has the compact intensity of poetry, where words and phrases are used in a very innovative and evocative manner not unlike the sort of inventive language of Annie Prouix's 'The Shipping News'! Having travelled to and fro across the United States and Canada by Greyhound in the seventies, I can relate to much of the atmosphere the author recreates (though thankfully my journeys were in August and not snowbound!)"

(Paul Harrison, Devon, England)

LIMBERLOST III THE PREQUEL – 2016

BLISS DIDN'T JUST want handsome 'working' gals who were seldom good for nothin' else except their looks and their horizontality. Sure, she wanted girls who were not physically repulsive, but moreover she sought out girls who were of 'satisfactory size'; girls who were in fine fettle and kind of well-fortified. Bliss referred to them as 'gristly' girls who were not amiss to handling a demanding days grind and some cussing too, if it alleviated the days burden for them. She wanted plain stitching, wood splitting, bread yeasting girls and more significantly she didn't want pie in the sky females who were waiting to marry a nonsensical knight errant – or more especially a random Polish troubadour!

Bliss was philosophical about her new venture and chewed over to herself how peculiar it all was; the to-ing and fro-ing of all those perfidious spouses. Straight-faced and somewhat astonished, she contended that the one unique characteristic about those men who have a taste for wallowing in a cesspool, is that they cannot be made much dirtier by doing it!

With the advent of World War II and Anville having a military establishment close by, Bliss deemed it necessary to arrange regular visits from Anville's Social Protection Officer, Betty Andersen. Withal Bliss was highly regarded for the virtuous quality of her girls and she didn't digest the thought of venereal disease and such disrupting her cash crop.

In any event 10 joyful years of fuddled fornication, just justifiably scampered by so quickly, and for et al and Bliss it was 10 most effectual and beneficial years indeed.

But everything runs its course and one day God, out of the blue, realised just how much Bliss loved her fellow man and kindly asked if she would team up with him. I guess he wanted to give the other side of heaven a taster of Bliss' hospitality! I can picture her there right now wearing silver-coated underwear beneath her cotton twill jeans!

As the afternoon gives up the sun
the shadows lengthened one by one
when God invited Bliss to dance
to give the other side a chance.
How those Sunday bells rang out loud
Big men in suits were singing proud

The mind is such an uncannily queer junkyard. It remembers the names of candy bars but cannot remember the Gettysburg Address. It remembers Frank Sinatra's middle name but cannot recall the day a best friend died.

Appreciation for Limberlost III The Prequel – 2016

"Sensitive, emotional and profound – Ricky Dale enjoys an easy and fluid writing style and a sure ear for the rhythms of contemporary speech; dialogue, in particular internal, is well crafted."

(Athena Press, London, England – affiliated in the USA)

CLOUDBURST – 2019

IT WAS STILL fairly early in the morning and small business guys were opening up their joints for the day. No one was about to take any notice of two young Yanks as they made their way along Blackfriars Road to the Southbank Centre. There was a garden that Sandra adored there, an actual authentic garden right in the centre of London, filled with wild flowers, vegetable patches... and a bar!

A big, six-foot two guy with straw coloured hair and a matching moustache (who they had christened 'Blondy' Swanson) met them at the entrance. "Did you chastise the scoundrel?" he smiled: "Sh-h-h!" replied Sandra "I seem to remember we did."

'Blondy' Swanson was a well respected and totally irreligious boss! Yet later that year it was reported that His Holiness Pope John Paul II found time in the Vatican to clasp Swanson's hands fervently between his own which could only be described as an embrace. The Holy Father's attention was always on the ball – justifiably so!

God's Banker – Roberto Calvi was found hanging from Blackfriars Bridge in 1982.

Appreciation for Cloudburst – 2019

My thoughts on Ricky Dale's Cloudburst book : I just finished the read...

> *"Cloudburst's edgy, controversial, simple yet complex narrative, is at times written with humorous undertones and at other times with such heartfelt badass emotion that it lightens up the darkness of the novel's nature and leaves its fictional reality up to one's own interpretation."*

(DJL – former publisher)

"Beautiful writing. This is a fabulous story, uniquely told in a very poetic style. I've never read anything quite like it. I'd recommend it to anyone. The writing seems to meander, but it never goes so far askew that it gets lost, more like a hazy, fantastical, escapist wander through another life. Highly recommended to anyone who wants something a bit different to the standard fare"

(Digital Electronics and data)

"Brilliant! A brilliant read, excellently written couldn't leave it alone"

(Amazon customer)

'THE HOUSE ON DUNDAS & VINE'

– is a semi-autobiographical/semi-fiction work in progress as at January 2021

1

GLORIA WAS A street car driver and I loved her. In those days I sang at a club downtown and each evening after my singing was done she always drove the last bus home. Often I would sit by the window just so as I could see her in the reflection.

I don't know what first drew me to her. Perhaps it was those sad dark eyes beneath the tinted bifocals she wore. It wasn't at all like I made a habit of falling in love with total strangers – withal at work I saw dozens of pretty girls who I never wanted to know – perhaps it was Gloria's yellow hair too?

I knew she had a good heart right from the start. If there were bicycles waiting at a crossing she would always let them go first.

I was undiscovered and alone until one zero temperature night it happened, she said…"Hello!"

It wasn't so long after that I gave her a candy bar and it wasn't so long after that she gave me a cigarette and a free ride home.

I did lie when I told her I was a salesman selling shoes and such. You see I didn't want her knowing that I worked at Duffy's – it is not a club with a good reputation!

I knew the bride when she used to rock n roll

About the Author

RICKY DALE WAS born in the breath-taking county of Devonshire, England and was subsequently raised in West Africa and Ontario, Canada.

He quit school at 14 years of age, borrowed £100 from his parents and sailed off on the ocean liner Franconia on its maiden voyage to Montreal.

Often he had tried out his singing voice at youth clubs and friend's parties and more recently in the school band and had quickly developed a palate for 'applause' and so, with that goal very much in mind, he set his sights on singing for a living in North America.

Ricky was quite a resourceful kid so it wasn't long before he had exaggerated his age and previous experience and began foot-slogging and auditioning in and around Montreal.

He was finally snapped up by *The Wilkinson Theatrical Agency* in Hamilton, Ontario. Ricky says "They hired me out to all manner of venues – clubs, bars, private parties. They really put me to work. I earned a weekly fixed sum of $52.75 – an absolute fortune compared to a kid's wage in England!"

By and by he began to grace the spotlight of many of the more eminent clubs across the province including the legendary Brant Inn in Burlington, Ontario. The fabulous Brant was renowned for bringing together hugely popular entertainers not only from Canada, but because of the Brant's location, also from across the border in the United States. Ricky once duetted with the sheer genius Danny Kaye and often with international crooners such as the great Johnnie Ray. "Those Brant years were definitely the ultimate years for me" he says.

After some time Ricky figured out it was time to return to his roots in Devon. During the ensuing years he established a group of innovative businesses in Falmouth, Torquay and Weymouth, with the intention of interconnecting their activities along the coast.

Whilst living in Canada Ricky had personally involved himself with the Native Americans and developed a profound curiosity into their culture and distinctive ways of life. In particular the all-important essence of their spiritual and metaphysical reasoning.

"I unearthed numerous parallels between the Native American tribes' beliefs and that of certain tribes in West Africa" he says. "The attempted transformation of these peoples' lives and culture by armies of white interlopers and the abominable chaos that has resulted are but the fruits of foreigners disobedience toward fundamental spiritual law."

"In some sad respects it isn't their fault; they are just too far removed from the formative process of it all. Inasmuch that long revered elements such as lightning, fire, wind and water, and even contagion are all crucial keys that some outsiders prefer to remain ignorant of. Similarly, they would find it difficult to swallow the suggestion of a bizarre occurrence being attributed to the action of the spirit!"

"And so, on the basis of all those powers that cannot be explained, my daughter advocated me stringing together a book systematically chronicling my intimate communications with the presumed sphere of the spiritual, but in any event a book about stuff that cannot necessarily be rationalised at first glance."

What bothered me about that suggestion is that I didn't want to assume responsibility (or control) over such a project workout. In all likelihood I would have probably taken up on it if for example my daughter had been ghost writing (no pun intended) the book for me.

And so that, dear reader, is why I put this novel together instead. It works for me only because I have been able to combine fiction with fact in the most non-discriminatory form.

"Fingers crossed! I hope you will find it overwhelmingly absorbing!"

Ricky Dale

Lightning Source UK Ltd.
Milton Keynes UK
UKHW020705051022
409964UK00019B/1504